A deadly
assignment
to protect
the President's
daughter leads
to a battle
between duty
and desire

Above All, HONOR

RADCLYffE

Praise for Radclyffe's Fiction

"...well-plotted...lovely romance...I couldn't turn the pages fast enough!" – Ann Bannon, author of *The Beebo Brinker Chronicles*.

"...well-honed storytelling skills...solid prose and sure-handedness of the narrative..." – Elizabeth Flynn, *Lambda Book Report*

"...a thoughtful and thought-provoking tale...deftly handled in nuanced and textured prose that is both intelligent and deeply personal. The sex is exciting, the story is daring, the characters are well-developed and interesting – in short, Radclyffe has once again pulled together all the ingredients of a genuine page-turner..." – Cameron Abbott, author of *To the Edge* and *An Inexpressible State of Grace*

"With ample angst, realistic and exciting medical emergencies, winsome secondary characters, and a sprinkling of humor...a terrific romance...one of the best I have read in the last three years. Highly recommended." – Author Lori L. Lake, Book Reviewer for the *Independent Gay Writer*

"Radclyffe employs...a lean, trim, and tight writing style...rich with meticulously developed characterizations and realistic dialogue..." – Arlene Germain, *Lambda Book Report*

"...one writer who creates believably great characters that are just as strong as mainstream publishing's Kay Scarpetta or Kinsey Milhone...If you're looking for a great romance, read anything by Radclyffe." – Sherry Stinson, editor, *Outlook Press*

Above All, HONOR

2004 Edition

by

RADCLY*ff*E

2004

ABOVE ALL, HONOR (REVISED EDITION)

© 2002 BY RADCLYFFE. ALL RIGHTS RESERVED.

ISBN 1-933110-04-X

THIS TRADE PAPERBACK ORIGINAL IS PUBLISHED BY:
BOLD STROKES BOOKS, INC., PHILADELPHIA, PA, USA

FIRST EDITION: JANUARY 2002
SECOND PRINTING: SEPTEMBER, 2004 BOLD STROKES BOOKS, INC.
THIRD PRINTING: DECEMBER, 2004 BOLD STROKES BOOKS, INC.

CREDITS
EXECUTIVE EDITOR: STACIA SEAMAN
PRODUCTION DESIGN: J. GREYSTONE
COVER DESIGN BY SHERI (GRAPHICARTIST2020@HOTMAIL.COM)

By the Author

Romances

Safe Harbor	Tomorrow's Promise
Beyond the Breakwater	Passion's Bright Fury
Innocent Hearts	Love's Masquerade
Love's Melody Lost	shadowland
Love's Tender Warriors	Fated Love

Honor Series

Above All, Honor

Honor Bound

Love & Honor

Honor Guards

Justice Series

A Matter of Trust (prequel)

Shield of Justice

In Pursuit of Justice

Justice in the Shadows

Change Of Pace: *Erotic Interludes*
(A Short Story Collection)

Acknowledgements

The release of the original version of this book marked my first experience with these characters as well as one of my earliest forays into the world of publication. I've learned a great deal more about the characters since then, having published a sequel, *Honor Bound*, and written a third in the series, *Love and Honor*, to be published in the upcoming year. I've also come to appreciate a bit more about the complexities of making a book a complete reading experience. I am extremely happy to have had the opportunity to provide more of Cam, Blair, and the team's history in this revised, expanded edition.

Many thanks to Athos, my friend and supporter since my very first days of posting web fiction, for proofing the manuscript; to HS, for maintaining the Radlist and keeping my readers updated; to Jane, JB, and Tomboy for beta reading my works-in-progress.

I am indebted to Stacia Seaman for her usual excellent job of editing as well as for working cheerfully with severe time constraints. Any errors or inconsistencies that remain are mine alone.

I don't have enough praise for the superb artwork that Sheri provides in creating these covers. I can only say thank you from the heart for making me look so good.

Lee remains the rock upon which my world stands. *Amo te.*

For Lee,

For Each Word

CHAPTER ONE

"I don't want this assignment."

"You don't have a choice."

"This isn't even my area." Her voice was deep and forceful, and, at the moment, riding the razor edge of control. Her eyes were winter gray, deadly cold. "I'm an investigator, not a goddamned baby-sitter."

"You've been selected by the security council. They think you're the best one to head up the detail." Assistant Director Stewart Carlisle regarded her impassively. He'd expected this reaction. She was a seasoned field agent with more than a decade's experience, and, despite recent events, a highly effective one. She'd be in line for an assistant director's position if she ever learned to play the game. That thought almost made him smile. *Not very likely.*

"With all due respect, *sir*, I *am* a senior agent. I should have some say regarding my assignments."

She was right; they both knew it. He studied the tall, trim, dark-haired agent silently. She was thinner than the last time he had seen her, and there was a new hardness in her dark eyes. She stared at him in thinly disguised challenge, anger simmering very near the surface. The folder on his desk held her service record, and he knew every word by heart. It was flawless, exemplary in every way. It told the crucial facts, and none of the story. No one had ever known the whole story, and now they never would. Because she wasn't talking, and no one really wanted her to. What everyone wanted was to get on with business as usual, and it was his job to see that that happened.

"The directive was clear," Carlisle said flatly. "The decision is not negotiable."

"Any rookie could do it," she seethed through clenched teeth. *You're wrong. But I expect you'll discover that soon enough.*

"Is this some kind of punishment?" She was skirting the edge of insubordination. She knew it, and she didn't care. There wasn't a thing anyone could do to her that could hurt her any longer. Except maybe bury her in a bullshit detail like this. She needed a field assignment—something that would consume her energy, something that would exhaust her mind, something that would obliterate her memories. "A little late for that, don't you think?"

"Most people would consider this a top post."

"Not the people on my side of the street." Her laugh was brittle. "Is it the injury? Do they think I'm not fit for *real* duty?"

"Are you?"

"Absolutely. I've been released from rehab. I've passed the mandatory psych eval." Her leg still wasn't quite right, she couldn't sleep, and most of the time all she felt was empty, but he didn't need to know that. "I'm ready."

"Good. I'm glad to hear it. You start tomorrow. I suggest you review the available reports from the current commander before you leave for New York."

"Damn it, Stewart. You know I don't deserve this!"

"This has nothing to do with you, Agent. That will be all."

When she turned away, stiff with rage, he felt a wave of sympathy. She *did* deserve more from them than an assignment that to her could only seem like a demotion. He had no doubt she would give her best; she always did. What he wondered was where she would put her anger.

❖

"Booth seven is free," the firearms supervisor informed her.

She nodded and grabbed a pair of protective ear mufflers as she walked through the small office to the long corridor that opened into the individual firing stations. She wore a gray T-shirt and navy sweatpants from her two-hour workout at the gym, and the back of her shirt was still wet with sweat. The small bag she carried held her service automatic and ammunition. She looked neither right nor left as she strode rapidly toward the narrow glass enclosure.

There was a row of buttons that allowed her to set the target type and distance. She began with a medium-range standard human form and fired off a clip at an easy pace, alternating between clusters in the mid-torso and head. As she rhythmically squeezed the trigger, her mind slowly emptied of emotion until all she felt was the recoil of her weapon and the measured beat of her heart. When her anger over an assignment that she had no desire to undertake and couldn't avoid slowly abated, she moved the target fifty feet farther away. Accuracy demanded even greater concentration, and as she began to fire in faster, tighter bursts, the ever-present vestiges of longing and loss gradually faded.

By the time she had moved the smallest target to its farthest distance, she felt absolutely nothing.

❖

Fresh from the shower, she walked naked across the carpeted living room to the bar. Her apartment was on the top floor, and the floor-to-ceiling windows were uncovered, exposing the night skyline of Washington, D.C. The view was breathtaking. She poured an inch of single malt Scotch into a heavy crystal rock glass and leaned against the bar, staring at the city lights mingling with the stars. There had been a time when this vision had moved her with its piercing beauty. There had been many nights when she had allowed the tensions of the day to drift away into that great expanse of flickering light, feeling the world settle back into some kind of order. It was often the last thing she saw before she slipped into bed, but then she hadn't been alone.

Now when she looked out the window, she saw the past reflected back at her. Unchangeable, immutable, unforgiving. She had no desire to contemplate what she couldn't undo. She had no desire to think at all. Not tonight. She glanced at the clock. Soon she wouldn't have to.

She reached for the gray silk robe from the back of a chair when a knock sounded at the door. She had a flight to New York in five hours, and a meeting with her new team at 8:00. She still needed to review the dossier that had been delivered by courier that evening. She didn't have much time, and she knew she wouldn't sleep.

She glanced at the clock again as she crossed to the door. It was 1:00 a.m. Her visitor was punctual; she always was. She opened the door to admit a woman in her mid-thirties, expensively dressed in a beige linen suit, a silk shirt open to expose the swell of her breasts, and low-heeled, soft tan boots. Casually elegant. The woman greeted her with a familiar smile, brushing her blond hair back with a long elegant hand. "Hello."

"Hi." As she closed the door, she asked, "Can I get you something to drink?"

"That depends," the blond replied as she slipped her jacket off and laid it carefully across the back of a leather couch that faced the windows. "Are you in the mood for talking tonight?"

"I don't have much time."

"Then I'll have that drink another night," her guest replied softly. With a knowing gaze, she assessed the faint circles beneath normally clear gray eyes and noted the tightness along the sculpted jaw. "Sit down in front of the windows."

Wordlessly, the woman in gray dimmed the lights as she moved around to the sofa and sat as directed. The room was in near darkness now except for the shadows etched in the moonlight. She might have been one of them as she sipped her Scotch and watched the stars revolve overhead. She had been here before, in the still of the night, but not quite like this. Never quite so detached, so singularly isolated despite the warmth of the body just barely perceptible between her thighs. She was distantly aware of the gentle tug that loosened the belt at her waist and the soft parting of the silk that covered her. At the first light touch of fingers against her skin, she shivered involuntarily.

Eventually the teasing strokes over her taut abdomen and along her inner thighs became firmer, more insistent, demanding her attention. When the press of palms high on the inside of her legs bid her open, she arched toward the woman kneeling before her in the dark, tightening almost painfully as warm lips encircled her. Slow, practiced caresses of a velvet smooth tongue swept every image from her consciousness, eclipsing thought with near-agonizing pleasure. A groan escaped her as she dropped her head back against the couch, allowing the slowly building pressure to take her outside herself, beyond thought, past memory. The pounding of her heart grew loud in her ears as her breath came in short gasps, almost sobs. Eyes closed, she struggled to contain the exquisite, piercing ache centered in her clitoris, and failed. When the explosion began, ripping at her control, she slipped one hand into the soft blond hair, moaning deep in her throat. Trembling, helpless, for a few moments she was mercifully unaware.

❖

She walked the blond to the door and picked up a sealed envelope that rested on the table just inside the foyer. She handed it to her visitor, who took it wordlessly and slipped it into her purse.

"I'll be away for a while. I don't know how long."

"Will I see you again?"

"I don't know."

The blond studied the tall, handsome stranger she had met countless times in the dark hours of the night—in this room, in elegant hotel suites—in rooms that might be anywhere, or nowhere at all. She knew virtually nothing of the other woman's life, except what she gleaned from the confessions of her body. She knew the hard, lean muscles and the angry red scar on her thigh that was healing now, faded over the months since they had met. She knew the soft, sensitive places that left her gasping when touched. She wondered whose name the stranger called out when she came into the silence. She had never tried to find out, and she did not want to know now. Strangely, it was something else she wanted altogether. If this was to be their last meeting, she wanted to leave something of herself.

Breaking every rule, the blond said softly, "My name is Claire."

"Claire," the dark-eyed stranger whispered, the expression in her intense gaze unfathomable as she leaned close and kissed her for the first time. It was a brief, tender meeting of lips that spoke a greeting, or perhaps a goodbye. Then, breaking every rule, she said, "My name is Cameron."

When the door closed, leaving them to their separate lives, with their silent secrets, the lingering memory of that kiss was all that remained between them.

CHAPTER TWO

At 6:00 a.m., United States Secret Service Agent Cameron Roberts boarded a small jet bound for New York City. She wore her ID badge clipped to the breast pocket of her charcoal gabardine suit. She carried an overnight bag with a change of clothes and her computer. The rest of her belongings would follow on a separate flight and would be delivered to her new apartment in the Gramercy Park Hotel later that day by some member of her team. After four hours of deep sleep, undisturbed by dreams, she felt fresh and ready to work. That she didn't like her assignment was now a moot point and no longer concerned her. She had a job to do, and that was all that mattered.

The flight was only partially full. It was Saturday morning, and only a few government employees were traveling. She took a seat across the aisle from a burly blond man with a badge that proclaimed "FBI" in bold letters. She saw him study her own badge as she sat down. Female agents were no longer rare, but she still drew attention. She was used to it.

"Investigative division?" he questioned, referring to one of the two arms of the Secret Service, as the plane taxied down the runway.

She nearly said yes, then stopped herself quickly. For twelve years that had been true, but not any longer. With a shake of her head, she replied, "Protective."

"Anybody important?" he asked curiously.

"Aren't they all?"

He couldn't tell if she was joking, so he stifled a laugh. *And they say FBI agents are humorless. Jesus.*

She opened her laptop computer, subtly angling the screen away from him. He took the hint and opened a newspaper as she entered her password.

She entered the link to the USSS personnel division and brought up the bios on her new team. Nothing out of the ordinary. Four men and two women in addition to herself, most with more than five years experience in the field. All college educated, as were almost all agents except the rare few who came through military channels or some other unusual route. All had advanced emergency medical training, as had she, and all were expert marksman. Two of the men and one woman were married; there were one Hispanic and one African-American agent. She fixed a name to each face and exited the site.

Entering another protected password, she brought up the encrypted file she had downloaded the previous night.

```
Field Report, Fri 12/26/00, 21:30
Submitted by USSS Agent in Charge Daniel
Ryan

Subject: Blair Allison Powell
DOB: 12/31/1975
Residence: 310 Gramercy Park, PH New York
City, 10021
Phone: (212) 295-0566
Marital Status: Single
Occupation: Artist
Business address: NA

Code Name: Egret

Physical Description: WF, 5'8", 120 lbs.
Hair: Blond
Eyes: Blue.
Distinguishing marks: 2 cm scar right
eyebrow, 3 cm tattoo right posterior
shoulder (purple and blue labyris)
```

```
Education:  Dana  Hill  School,  Wellesley,
Mass
Choate Rosemary Prep, Wallingford, Conn
Paris Institute of Fine Arts

Medical Conditions: None
Allergies: None

Business Agent: Diane Bleeker
Romantic: Current - unverified
Last known: classified, FYEO file
Significant  relationships:  (SEE  ATTACHED
REPORTS)
Summary:     Standard     twenty-four-hour,
rotating   shift   surveillance.   Subject
schedule fluid, frequently unverifiable.
Communication link: Team commander only
per subject request. On-person com-links—
refused.
```

The file was bare-bones minimum, and Cam wondered what her predecessor wasn't willing to commit to hard copy. She'd find out soon enough. He was meeting her at the airport for a debriefing.

She sipped her coffee and slipped the thin folder that held the "Eyes Only" report on Egret's last known lover from her briefcase. She read it carefully, her expression betraying nothing. According to this, until eighteen months ago, the president's daughter had been having an affair with the wife of the French ambassador. For obvious reasons, knowledge of the relationship had been kept under deep cover, although rumors had floated in the security community for years about the sexual leanings of Blair Powell. Cam had heard them and, because it had nothing to do with her, dismissed them. Apparently, the rumors were a bit more than conjecture, and now she could no longer ignore them. Part of her job was to see that the details of the first daughter's personal life remained private and that to the rest of the world, rumors remained just that. Her task would be doubly hard if the subject refused to cooperate.

And if I'm reading between the lines of the field report correctly, the last commander found the president's daughter far from obliging.

She wondered briefly if *her* appointment as commander of the security detail assigned to Ms. Powell hadn't been due to her own sexual preferences. It wasn't a matter of record, of course, but no one really believed that anyone in the government's employ had any secrets. She had been careful, but certainly not paranoid, about her personal life. After the events of a year ago, she doubted there was much her superiors didn't know. Speculation was futile, and pointless. She knew for certain she didn't care.

She fed the file recounting the details of Blair Powell's love-life into the shredder at the front of the plane as she exited.

❖

"Sorry to transition on the run," Daniel Ryan remarked as they settled into a booth in the airport cafeteria. "I have to catch a flight out at 0800."

"No problem," Cam replied neutrally. She didn't know Ryan. She knew almost no one in the protective branch of the service, which might be either a blessing or a curse. She'd have fewer contacts if she needed behind-the-scenes assistance, but she'd also have less history with those above and below her. She'd been given this command, or more correctly, been forced to take it, and she intended to run it the way she saw fit. She'd owe no one, and that was just the way she liked it.

"Mac Phillips is the second in command and will basically be your aide, unless you decide you want someone else. He's a good communications man. He has the apartment building plans, evac routes, and hospital info ready to review with you as soon as you arrive. Your NYPD liaison is Captain Stacy Landers; she's Hostage Rescue. She usually interfaces with the police patrol division commander, Lieutenant Chuck Thayer, if Egret is traveling to some public function. Both good people. Otherwise, we cover her internally. Rotating shifts, eight-hour tours, with a primary agent assigned to her who is free to float if there's some unscheduled event."

"Uh-huh," Cam said casually. Everything he was telling her could have easily been relayed by anyone on the team. She was waiting for him to get to the point of this private meeting.

He watched her watching him. Her rep was that she was a real straight arrow. A by-the-book agent. She'd have to be to get this post. She certainly looked the part. Her thick dark hair was perfectly trimmed, neat around her ears, collar length in back; her suit was without a wrinkle and subtly tailored to her tight, trim build; she didn't display a hint of nerves or anything else, assessing him with intense, piercing gray eyes. The bio he'd been given showed she'd been advancing rapidly through the investigative unit. Why she'd been reassigned to the protective division was anybody's guess. Beyond that scant information, she was a cipher. He couldn't find anyone who had inside knowledge about her, and no one had heard even a whisper that she was anything other than an obsessively dedicated agent. He met her gaze and made a decision.

"Can we talk off the record here?"

"Go ahead," Cam responded. *It's about time.*

"Every day for the last six months I woke up wondering who I had pissed off to get this assignment," he said with a shake of his head. "Egret is practically impossible to protect because she doesn't want us around. She's been under some kind of protective watch since she was a kid, and she knows the ropes. She's a goddamned expert at misleading us, evading us, and generally humiliating us when it comes to surveillance. She's like Jekyll and Hyde."

He rubbed his face and made an effort to keep his voice even. "At public functions, she's fine—cooperative, even friendly. Privately, she does everything she can to make our job hell. She refuses to discuss her schedule with anyone except the team commander. Congratulations—now that's you."

His tone implied that was a dubious honor. Cam said nothing.

"Then," he continued darkly, "she changes plans without telling anyone. We almost never have time to adjust vehicle placement or equipment, so we're forced to shadow her on foot—which in New York City is a nightmare. She absolutely refuses to wear a microphone or any other tracking device, even on direct instruction from the president." He handed her two photographs. "Then there's this."

She studied the shots side by side. The first was a standard color publicity photo like dozens she'd seen of the president's daughter. The close-up depicted Blair Powell at the opening of the Reagan Building the previous year. As usual, she looked poised and confident. Her blond hair was swept back from her face, held with a silver clasp at the base of her neck. Her make-up was understated and flawless, serving only to accentuate the natural elegance of her sculpted face and clear, smooth skin. Her designer dress highlighted her sleek form, complementing both her athleticism and her subtle softness. She was, in a word, beautiful.

The second photo was a candid taken when the subject was unaware. It was grainy, suggesting it had been shot from a long-range unit through a telephoto lens. The details, however, were clear. The woman in the photo was exiting an apartment building, location unknown, and had been caught as she ran down the stairs to the street. She wore tight faded jeans and a white cotton tank top, short enough to expose an expanse of tight midriff. Her breasts, firm and well shaped, were clearly evident beneath the thin material and just as clearly unencumbered by a brassiere. The clothes displayed her long legs, sleek torso, and toned limbs with brazen explicitness. Her collar-length blond hair hung free around her face, mildly curly, looking as if she had simply run her hands through it in lieu of a comb. She wore no make-up and didn't look like she needed any. Even in the still photo, she exuded an energy that was palpable. She projected the sensuality of a jungle cat and looked about as dangerous. Upon casual observation, she bore almost no resemblance to the contained, refined woman in the first shot.

Cam handed him the photographs silently. It was his show.

"No one in the general public recognizes her like that, and sometimes it even takes us a minute or two. In that time, she can disappear into a crowd, walk into a restaurant unnoticed, or get into a cab without a fuss. That's why it's so easy for her to lose us. No one points a finger at her or runs after her trying to get an autograph."

"But you and your operatives still know what she looks like," Cam pointed out. "You can find her." That was obvious, and she wondered when he would get to the real issue.

He nodded agreement. "Sure we can. Most of the time. The problem is, we need to protect her privacy as well as her reputation." He ignored the slight lift in Cam's eyebrow at that line of bullshit. Blair Powell *had* no privacy. And they both knew it was the *president's* image they needed to keep untarnished. Any scandal regarding his daughter reflected on his parenting skills, and ultimately on his character. It wasn't necessarily a make-or-break issue, but every bit of bad press or acrimonious debate affected public opinion. Political fortunes had turned on less.

Blowing out a breath, he cut to the chase. "She's a lesbian. In certain situations, if we call attention to her, that's going to get out. She knows it, and she uses it."

"How so?"

"She frequents some of the gay bars. It's hard for me to put agents in there, even when they're undercover. I never know when she's going to duck into one. Plus, I don't exactly want to announce to everyone in the place that Blair Powell just walked in. She picks up women—women we have absolutely no way of identifying in the moment. We have no way to know where they might go, no way to put agents in place in advance. We are constantly running in second place hoping to God she doesn't get herself into trouble before we can get there."

"Is she promiscuous?" Cam asked evenly.

"She does better with women than I ever did," he remarked in frustration. "She doesn't have a steady girlfriend. I wish to hell she did. Then maybe we could keep track of her. She doesn't exactly sleep around, but she doesn't go long without sex either."

"What are you trying to tell me here, Agent Ryan?" Cam asked, tired of skirting the edges of the issue. "In addition to the fact that we have an uncooperative, high-profile subject with a very problematic lifestyle?"

"She's an angry animal in a cage, and you're the new zookeeper. She's been trying to escape for years, and when she does, someone is going to get hurt."

Cam inclined her head in agreement. It was a career breaker, and she could see why Ryan was glad to get out. If she had the luxury of empathizing with the first daughter, she would have felt deeply for her predicament. Blair Powell had lived with constant surveillance since her father had been elected vice president for two terms, and prior to that, when he had been governor of New York. Now that he was a newly seated president, she had at least three more years of even closer monitoring. She was a prisoner in all but name, and Cam doubted anyone could tolerate that for long. The political pressure to hide her sexuality surely made it even worse. But Blair Powell's happiness was not her responsibility, and she couldn't waste time or objectivity worrying about it.

"Someone may indeed get hurt," she responded. "I intend to see that it's not her."

❖

"Agent Roberts?" a handsome Brad Pitt look-alike inquired as Cam stepped off the elevator on the eighth floor of a brownstone apartment building that faced the south side of Gramercy Park. He extended his hand with a disarming smile. "I'm Mac Phillips. The others are inside the command post briefing room. Welcome to the Aerie."

"Agent Phillips." She took his outstretched hand, smiling at the play on "eagle's nest." "Cameron Roberts."

"Call me Mac, Commander."

"Done. What's on for this morning, Mac?"

She accompanied him into a large loft space that had been sectioned into work cubicles and equipment stations by shoulder-high particleboard partitions. The Secret Service's surveillance center occupied the entire floor directly below Blair Powell's penthouse suite. A small conference room enclosed by glass filled the far corner. As they approached the group of people seated within, Phillips consulted a printout in his hand.

"Intro and weekly briefing now. You are scheduled to meet with Egret at 1100 in the penthouse." He caught her faint expression of surprise and shrugged. "She won't talk to any of us. She says if she must discuss her plans, it will only be once, and with the team commander."

"It's her prerogative," Cam remarked with no inflection. As she walked, she made careful note of the banks of video monitors, multi-cassette recorders, computer simulators, and a large grid of New York City, digitally indexed and showing real-time placement of police vehicles. It was the same array of equipment used to monitor the White House and surrounds, and for the same reason. The president was vulnerable through his family. To avoid the appearance of that vulnerability, the first family needed to be shown living as normal a life as possible, and that did not include being shuttled about by armed guards. Hence, their protection needed to be provided at a distance, with as little visibility as possible. The semblance of freedom was a ruse they all conspired to perpetuate— everyone, apparently, except Blair Powell.

Phillips held the conference door open for her, and she strode through without a second's hesitation. This was her field to command.

"Good morning, people. I am Cameron Roberts." She stood at the head of the oblong table and glanced at each face, making brief eye contact with everyone, and allowing them a good look at her. When she was certain she had everyone's attention, she sat, stating briskly, "You have one hour to tell me everything I need to know about this operation, and everything you *don't* think I need to know as well. Let's get started."

At the end of an hour during which Cam listened, questioned, and issued a few directives, the agents who constituted her team sensed there was a new game in town. Everyone present took their responsibility seriously, for the sake of their future employment if for no other reason, and each had felt the frustration voiced earlier by the departing team commander. That dissatisfaction was heightened by the fact that they disliked Blair Powell, although none of them would ever say so, even to each other. In the six months that the team had been charged with the protection of the first daughter, the obstructive, uncooperative attitude of Blair Powell had subtly undermined the confidence of the operatives. An hour with Cameron Roberts provided them with the first jolt of optimism they'd felt in weeks.

"Allow me to summarize," Cam said as she stood and walked to the window looking down on the postage-stamp-sized private garden that formed the heart of Gramercy Park. As she watched, an elderly woman unlocked the gate in the wrought-iron fence that surrounded the park. When she spoke again, her back was to the room, but her voice was clearly audible. "Ms. Powell resents our intrusion into her life. She resents our presence in every public and private moment of her day. Undoubtedly, she resents our observation of her personal liaisons and romantic encounters. I, for one, don't blame her."

She turned to the group with a small shrug. "The fact that Ms. Powell does not welcome our presence is immaterial. Our job is to see that she is able to carry on her life with the maximum degree of security possible, no matter where she is, or what she's doing, with the maximum degree of privacy achievable. She has decided to make this a game. We have to play, and, more importantly, we have to win. We don't get to throw in the towel or call foul if she changes the rules."

Every eye was on her as she placed her palms on the table and leaned forward. Her gaze was hard, her tone uncompromising as she finished, "There are no rain-outs. We can't expect her to help us win. We have to do that for ourselves. That's what we're getting paid for."

She smiled faintly as she took her seat again, suddenly understanding at least one of the reasons she had been given this assignment. "Remember that she is an uncooperative subject. Don't expect her to make your job easy; don't expect her to smile and say good morning. She has made it clear she does not want us around. She is not going to invite us along. We will switch from protective surveillance methods to investigative tactics, starting now. If she can't see you, it will be harder for her to lose you."

She looked pointedly at each of her agents, seeing them as Blair Powell must see them. Ivy League starched, polished and presentable. About as obvious as the proverbial bulls in the china shop.

"You need to be *with* her in order to protect her, so you've got to fit in where she travels. You have to function essentially undercover. Except at scheduled public functions where Ms. Powell is acting in some official capacity, no suits, no ties, no skirts. Street clothes, preferably something appropriate for the type of locales she is known to frequent."

She saw the slight stiffening of a few shoulders and continued unperturbed. It was time to stop circling the primary problem. "For you men, I think a slightly longer hair length would be helpful for starters. It's time for you to stop looking like cops." She sipped the last of her coffee, gathering her papers with the other hand. "A little research might also be in order. I want a summary of every gay bar and restaurant in New York City. Hours of operation, type of clientele, traffic patterns in the area, et cetera. Start with the ones you know she's been to. Have it on my desk before the day is out. Know your subject, ladies and gentlemen, and you have won the first point."

Everyone relaxed slightly as she pulled open the door to the conference room. She paused at the sill, turning back casually.

"By the way, Mac, does she know about the video equipment inside her apartment?"

He looked at her in surprise. *How had she noticed* that *on a quick walk through the monitoring section?*

"I doubt it," he said quietly. *If she were aware of the micro-cameras mounted in the ceiling of her loft, she would hardly be walking around nude the way she does.*

"Turn them off," Cam said flatly. "Video the elevator, the building exits, fire escapes, and garage only."

"Uh, Commander, we had specific directives from the White Hou—"

"Disable them. On my responsibility."

With that, she was gone, leaving them to wonder where one got the balls to countermand a direct order from the White House chief of staff.

CHAPTER THREE

At precisely 1100, Cam keyed the elevator to the penthouse and, a moment later, exited into a small foyer. Opposite her a carved oak door was set into panels of the same highly polished wood. The wallpaper on the other two walls adjoining the lift was an intricately patterned and luxuriously textured cream fabric above dark oak wainscoting. A small table bearing a thin crystal vase with a spray of fresh flowers sat beside the door. The effect was warm and sensual.

Cam rang the bell and waited.

Blair Powell opened the door a moment later, and Cam automatically made one swift, sweeping visual assessment. The first daughter's hair was wet from the shower, casually finger-combed and falling freely around her face. She wore a loosely belted blue silk robe that came to mid-thigh. Her legs were bare, and Cam knew that she was naked beneath the thin material. The front gaped just enough to reveal the soft inner curves of both breasts, and the faint impression of her nipples was clear. There was a trace of jasmine floating in the air.

Cam was assaulted with the seething sensuality she had sensed in the photograph Ryan had shown her earlier, a sensation so powerful as to be nearly tangible. Her skin prickled, and she brought her gaze carefully back to eye level. In a neutral tone, she said, "I'm Agent Roberts, Ms. Powell. I'll come back when you're ready for the briefing. If you would just call the command room—"

"I won't be available later," Blair interrupted, intently appraising the current commander assigned with her care. This one was definitely a surprise. She wore the requisite suit, much better cut than most—imported material, too. The impeccable tailoring hid any hint of a bulge from the shoulder holster. Her black hair was fashionably styled in a roguishly faux-masculine cut. The charcoal double-breasted jacket was open to expose a fine white linen shirt that hugged a well-developed chest and trim waist. The belted trousers were streamlined to tightly muscled thighs. With her deep gray eyes and chiseled features, Cameron Roberts was a remarkably attractive package. In addition, the commander was either unimpeachably heterosexual or exactly what she appeared to be—a lesbian who didn't care who knew it.

Blair was intrigued.

"It's either now or next week," the first daughter continued, enjoying her control. There was no way the new commander could wait even a few hours to discuss her schedule, and Blair knew it.

"Now would be fine," Cam acquiesced graciously. She didn't want a power struggle over trivial issues. She had no need to prove herself that way.

Blair stepped slightly aside, motioning Cam into the high-ceilinged open loft space. She smiled as Cam carefully avoided brushing against her. *All business*, she thought to herself.

"Do you have a first name, Agent Roberts?" Blair asked as she crossed to the kitchen area. A breakfast bar flanked by tall stools on one side separated the cooking space from the large living room. She leaned down to pull two cups from the shelves under the island, quite aware that the movement afforded a clear view into her dressing gown.

"Cameron," Cam replied, keeping her face and voice expressionless. Her mind registered the striking perfection of the younger woman's body. The image of her soft, pink-nippled breasts was now indelibly implanted in her memory. She was being taunted, that much was clear. What she didn't know was why.

Blair straightened slowly, searching for a reaction in the handsome agent's face. She was curious when she found none.

"Cameron," she breathed huskily. "That's nice. You can call me Blair."

"I'll try not to take too much of your time, Ms. Powell," Cam continued, outwardly appearing unperturbed while inwardly she worked to banish the unexpected disquiet the woman's physical appeal invoked. "If we could just review your plans for the week, I can leave you to your day."

Blair stared at her, undisguised anger suddenly seething in her blue eyes. "Don't patronize me, Agent Roberts. We both know you won't be *leaving* me to anything at all."

Cam nodded assent. "Forgive me, I didn't mean it that way. Of course, I can't. But I can make my presence and that of my people as unintrusive as possible."

"Oh, really? That would be novel." Blair was secretly surprised by the agent's conciliatory approach. That was a new tactic. Usually the team commanders tried to bully her with threats of unfavorable reports to her father, as if she were an unruly child whose after-school privileges could be taken away. Either that, or they *promised* her privacy while tightening the net around her the moment she cooperated. She had absolutely no reason to believe this one, despite the sincerity in her intense gray eyes.

"Coffee, Commander?" Blair walked around the island carrying the coffee until she was next to Cam. She reached to put the cups on the counter, intentionally brushing against the other woman as she did.

"Thank you." Cam didn't flinch at the contact, although her body registered the pressure of Blair's breasts against her arm and the heat of a naked thigh against her leg. She was annoyed by the twitch of arousal that occurred entirely involuntarily. She consciously kept her breathing light and steady.

She knows about the video cameras. That's why she's playing with me.

Putting the team commander in an embarrassing position on tape might conceivably benefit the first daughter at some point, or it just might be her idea of a game. Either way, the agent pitied Daniel Ryan. Blair Powell was a powerfully desirable woman, and if such attractions still interested Cam, it might have been a problem. But Blair had no way of knowing that despite the reflex arousal she provoked, Cam was immune to even *her* undeniable sexual allure.

"Anything else I can get you?" Blair murmured, deliberately pressing closer.

Cam allowed the moment of contact to linger long enough to make it clear she was aware of it, and undisturbed by it. She'd gotten quite a lot of practice in the last six months saying no to attractive women. Then she stepped away, reached into her inside jacket pocket for the computer log Mac had provided her, and held it up between them.

"The schedule?" she said softly.

Blair stared at her, color rising to her face. She had just been rebuked, subtly, but very definitely. Rejection from women was a new and quite unwelcome experience. She'd never been as blatantly provocative with Daniel Ryan, but she had sensed his discomfort whenever they were alone, and she knew she had an effect on him. She never would have slept with him, even *had* he responded to her small seductions. It was satisfying enough to know that she'd at least thrown him off stride. Apparently that was not going to be the case with her new commander, and that was not welcome news. If she must have a jailer, she wanted it to be one *she* commanded. Cameron Roberts's cool, aloof manner only heightened her desire to crack that perfect self-control.

"The *schedule*. Yes, let's get that over with," Blair responded with irritation, taking her coffee and moving into the sitting area.

Cam followed, noting the large work area in the far corner of the loft. Easels stood open holding canvases in various stages of completion, and other works leaned against every surface. Sunlight streamed through the skylights, illuminating the uncovered works. From the brief glimpse she got, it appeared that Blair Powell deserved her reputation as a serious artist. Cam took a seat across from Blair on one of two facing leather sofas. Blair tucked her legs under her as she curled gracefully into the cushions. Cam noted abstractly that the president's daughter was much more beautiful in her unconscious moments than when she used her considerable sexual power as a weapon. In the next instant, her mind had returned to the work at hand.

"I have you at a gallery opening uptown tomorrow, dinner at the White House New Year's Eve, and attending the Macy's parade back here in Manhattan with the mayor the next day," Cam read from the schedule. She looked to Blair for confirmation.

"Busy week," Blair muttered tersely. "That seems to be it. Are we done?"

Cam regarded her thoughtfully. She would have hated such intrusion, too, but there was nothing to be done about it. The fact that Blair Powell did not choose this life—it wasn't her, after all, who had run for public office—was beside the point. And the hard part was yet to come.

"What about your personal plans?" Cam asked, her eyes steady on Blair's face. She would not apologize for what she needed to do, and she wanted it clear that she would not compromise her own responsibility *or* Blair's safety because of Blair's dislike for the situation.

"I don't have any," Blair responded lightly.

Cam leaned back, tossing the schedule aside. She smiled faintly. "I need to know anything you have planned—dinner engagements, a date for drinks, that sort of thing. If you don't know now, I'll need you to tell me as things come up. All you have to do is check in with the command post."

"I know all this, Agent Roberts," Blair said testily.

"Yes, but apparently you're not fond of the routine."

"Would you be?"

"That's not the point. You are the daughter of the president of the United States. You don't need me to tell you what that means. Please let us do our jobs, and I promise you we will be as discreet as we can be."

"Do you expect me to tell you when I plan on a sexual liaison too?" Blair asked bluntly.

"I don't need to know *what* you're doing so much as where you're doing it," Cam responded smoothly. She knew Blair was trying to get her to back off, and she could not relent now. "It would be preferable if you would inform us when you planned to stay the night somewhere other than here, for example. As you know, we need to plan evac routes, among other things."

"And if I don't *know* where I'll be staying the night?" Blair looked for some reaction. Nothing but that unwavering gaze.

"Then I'll improvise." Cam took a breath. "One more thing. It's critical that I know with whom you'll be spending your time. Security is the priority, Ms. Powell. Unless it's someone you know well, and sometimes not even then, we cannot be assured of your safety. Everyone you spend time with needs clearance."

"You're joking."

"No, I'm not."

"What if I don't know them?" Blair's voice held challenge, and for an instant, bitterness.

"Then I would ask that you allow us to protect you at close range."

"Now *that* would be cozy." Blair leaned her head to one side and smiled lazily. "Into threesomes, Commander?"

Cam almost grinned, but she couldn't allow Blair to see it. "Private liaisons are particularly difficult for us, especially with unknown subjects, but I'll do my best to ensure discretion."

"You're a lot more direct than your predecessors, Commander. Aren't you afraid I'll complain about you? You could end up guarding some minor foreign diplomat on their tour of the Capitol, you know." Her tone was caustic, but she studied Cam with guarded respect. The new commander was definitely in a class of her own. Impossible to shock and clearly not intimidated by her. A refreshing change, but much more of a challenge than the others.

Cam did laugh then. "Ms. Powell, some people would consider that a plum assignment."

"Compared to this, you mean?"

"No, not necessarily." Cam stood, refusing to be provoked. "It was a pleasure to meet you, Ms. Powell. Please call me at any time if there is anything you wish to discuss. I would like to review your itinerary each day. Let the command room know when it will be convenient for you to meet with me, and please keep us advised of your plans."

"Oh, absolutely," Blair responded with a smile, her tone implying just how little that request meant to her. She remained seated as Cam left the room, thinking how attractive her tight, graceful body might be under other circumstances

❖

Mac Phillips looked up, raising an eyebrow slightly in inquiry, as his new boss walked into the command center. She appeared pensive but displayed none of the thinly veiled discomfort Ryan tried to hide after one of his encounters with Egret. But then Mac didn't expect Roberts to reveal anything. He couldn't remember the last time he had met anyone quite so impenetrable. Apparently, this was going to be a need-to-know operation.

"Anything unexpected?" he asked as she joined him.

"Not so far." Cam settled a hip onto the edge of the work counter. "The public functions are as outlined. For the gallery opening tomorrow, I'll be inside with the day team. Have two people with the car outside. That means the afternoon and evening shift will split the extra duty."

He made a note. "Right."

"We can use some of the White House detail for the dinner at the White House on New Year's Eve. Have one team stay here to meet her plane when she returns for the parade. Give the rest leave." She ran a hand through her hair, mentally ticking off points of procedure. "Make sure the ground team has reviewed the route and confirmed the municipal security placements *before* Egret lands on New Year's Day. We'll be on a tight schedule once we touch down at Triboro, and I don't want any last-minute adjustments."

"Done," he responded. He found her clear command attitude refreshing. He'd been impressed by the unspoken respect for Egret's position that she'd voiced in the meeting earlier, too. That and her firm position that they were there to protect the president's daughter, not have an easy time, was a welcome change. The undercurrent of dissatisfaction and criticism that had been the daily fare under the last command had been wearing on him. If she could turn that around, he was all for her.

"All of that is standard, Mac. In the future you can draw up the duty rosters. Just be sure I get a hard copy of who will be where."

"Yes, ma'am." He waited, wondering how she was going to deal with the real problem.

"Ms. Powell will not confirm any personal plans, which puts us in a reactive mode. I do not want her to get away from us, especially not now. I have a feeling she'll be testing our new command." She grimaced faintly. *Testing me.*

Mac nodded agreement. "More than likely. The problem is, she's completely unpredictable."

"She is going to move, you can be sure of that. Keep a car accessible in case she grabs a cab and have someone ready for foot pursuit, preferably a woman. If she goes to a gay bar, it might be easier if we have a woman on the inside."

"We've had lousy luck so far," Mac remarked. "Half the time we lose her in transit."

"That is no longer acceptable." Cam stood, stretching her cramped shoulders. "I'm going home. Page me the minute she steps out her door."

"Until what time?" Mac asked as he prepared to make a note.

"*Any* time," she said with finality. "If she isn't in her apartment, I want to know about it."

"Yes, ma'am," Mac responded crisply. He watched her glance once around the room, as if assuring herself that all was in order, before she left. He had a feeling Egret was in for a surprise, and he was looking forward to seeing it.

❖

As Cam walked through her new apartment to the shower, she stripped, eager to wash away the effects of her foreshortened night and early-morning flight. Eager also to cleanse the residue of her first meeting with her new charge from her mind *and* body. Unfortunately, the second goal was difficult to attain.

The cool spray refreshed her physically, but did little to ease the disquiet left from her briefing with Blair Powell. It was not just the younger woman's confrontational manner that had affected her, or even her attempts at seduction. That was clearly a game to the first daughter. It was her own reaction that angered her. She'd been unwillingly aroused, and however unbidden, she felt betrayed by the physical response. Worse, she'd been aware of the insistent pulse of stimulation long after she'd left Egret's apartment. Even the shower hadn't completely eased the heaviness of unappeased arousal.

With an irritated shake of her head, Cam pulled on running pants and a T-shirt. *Christ, I can hardly be expected to control my involuntary nervous system. And here in New York there's no discreet way to relieve it. I'll just have to run it off. It sure as hell won't be the first time.*

❖

Blair Powell stood at one of the floor-to-ceiling windows of her penthouse loft, watching the busy streets below. She recognized Cameron Roberts immediately when she ran lightly down the steps of her brownstone and began to jog toward Central Park. Even though Cam very quickly disappeared into the crowds, the afterimage of her lean form lingered in Blair's mind. She'd been thinking about her ever since their briefing that morning. As expected, the new commander had been all business, but Blair had sensed something different in this one. For an instant, when Roberts had been laying out the ground rules in her straightforward fashion, it had seemed like she really cared. Not just about the job, but about Blair.

Yeah, right. What she cares about is what they all care about. Good status reports.

She reached for the phone on a nearby end table and then hesitated before dialing. In all likelihood, the agents downstairs would record the call, even if they didn't actually listen in. Ordinarily, she didn't care, but this wasn't a conversation she wanted recorded. She switched to her cell phone and punched in a number from memory.

"Hey, you," she said with a smile in her voice when the line was picked up on the second ring. "I knew you'd be working even though it's Saturday afternoon. Still trying to be the youngest assistant director?…Uh-huh…Oh, yeah, sure." Blair listened for a moment, and then laughed. "Of course I need a favor! Background check—a Cameron Roberts. Listen, this might be a tough one. She's Secret Service…Yes, I know how much you're sacrificing. Just get me whatever you can. Call me as soon as you have something, okay? And hey—I know I owe you, really…What?…Not in this lifetime, you won't."

As she replaced the receiver, she contemplated calling downstairs to advise the team of her change in plans. But then again, why alter the routine now? The requests of her security chief had never mattered to her before. Still thinking of the intensity in Cameron Roberts's dark eyes, she slipped into a brown leather bomber jacket and left her apartment.

❖

The pager clipped to the waistband of the small pack Cam wore beeped just as she completed her first lap around the Central Park Reservoir. She dug out her cell phone, punching numbers with barely a break in stride.

"Roberts."

"Egret's on the move."

"Destination?"

"Unknown, ma'am."

"Are we covering?"

"So far. She's on foot, and we have her in visual."

"Good. Don't attempt to make contact. Just stay with her. I'll be back to base in twenty minutes. Have a car ready."

"Very good, Commander."

"And Fielding?" Cam snapped as she picked up her pace, threading her way around strollers and gawking tourists as she ran.

"Yes, ma'am?"

"Tell them not to lose her."

"Yes, ma'am."

Please, God, don't let us fuck up the first day, Agent John Fielding thought as he relayed his commander's instructions to the Secret Service agents in pursuit of the president's daughter.

❖

"Where is she?" Cam asked without preamble as she dumped her pack onto her bed and kicked off her running shoes. With the phone cradled against her shoulder, she pushed down her sweat-dampened navy pants, stepped free, and tugged up her T-shirt.

"At the Soho Gym," Fielding replied with obvious relief.

"Do you have visual confirmation of that?"

"Yes, ma'am. Paula Stark is inside."

Stark. An image came to mind. *Short dark hair, athletic build—youngest member of the team.* Cam relaxed minimally. "Good, then she's covered for the moment. I'm going to shower and change. If Egret moves again before I check in, call me."

Twenty minutes later Cam sat across the street from the Soho Gym watching the entrance. A metallic blue Ford idling diagonally opposite her held two Secret Service agents doing the same thing. She didn't think they were aware of her. She wasn't watching them. She trusted her agents for this type of routine surveillance. She was there because she wanted to get a sense of Blair Powell. She wanted to know where she ate, where she shopped, where she went for entertainment, and where she spent her evenings. Then she would begin to feel she could protect her.

Four hours later, Cam was beginning to fill in some of the blanks. From a distance, she had observed Blair dine with an exquisitely beautiful woman in a small Italian restaurant in the West Village. From there, the two had walked a few blocks to a neighborhood gay bar. Cam followed slowly in the car. They had taken their time along the way—window-shopping, browsing through a bookstore, purchasing espresso from a curbside stand, and perusing the display at an antique store. As they walked, Blair touched the woman occasionally—a palm on the small of her back, a brush of fingertips across the top of her hand.

Cam judged the movements to be friendly, but not especially intimate. If it was a date, it was a casual one, or else Blair Powell was fairly reserved. Cam smiled to herself, recalling Ryan's assessment of the president's daughter and her ways with women. *Casual* hadn't been the impression he'd given. And Blair Powell had been anything but reserved with *her* that morning. Remembering the brush of firm breasts against her arm, she felt a brief spasm of renewed arousal. *Jesus Christ, what is the matter with me?*

Annoyed, Cam focused on the bar across from where she sat. The two women were in there now, and so was one of her agents. She didn't really care if Blair saw him. The presence of the Secret Service should be anticipated. Cam had simply instructed him to keep his distance and not to intrude upon them. Time passed, and he had little to report.

It was well after midnight, Cam was beat, and she considered calling it a night. It didn't look like this was anything more than an evening out for Blair Powell, and the team assigned to shadow her seemed to have things under control. She was reaching for her radio to check out when she spotted Blair's companion hurry from the bar and hail a cab. Instantly alert, she keyed in the frequency of the agent in the bar.

"Young, this is Roberts. Do you have Egret in visual?"

"Negative. She's in the restroom."

Cam switched channels. "Stark—get in there and check out that restroom."

"I'm on it," the female agent replied as she exited the car parked just down the street from the small corner bar.

The moments passed slowly until Cam's earpiece crackled to life.

"She's not in here, Commander," Stark announced.

"Recheck the entire bar. If she's not inside, start a sweep of the surrounding area. She's on foot, at least for now." Cam punched in the numbers of the command center on her cell phone as she simultaneously disengaged the radio. "Fielding, give me the addresses of all gay bars in a twenty-block radius of this location—start with known locales first, particularly any Egret has frequented recently."

While Cam waited for the computer to produce the information, she considered the situation. Blair had intentionally evaded them, which was not all that hard to do since they weren't guarding her with the kind of manpower a criminal surveillance would demand. That was because Blair was supposed to be a friendly protectee. Now that the first daughter was out of their range, she was at potential risk for kidnapping, or if documented in some compromising circumstance, for blackmail. The fact that she was not easily identifiable as the president's daughter was the only thing they had going for them. It was going to be a long, tense night until they found her.

"I've got that list for you, Commander," Fielding said as he came on line.

"Go," she said, her right hand on the small terminal in the central console. When the printout emerged, she scanned in quickly. There were six potentials in the immediate area. "Get Mac Phillips in to coordinate the teams. I'm going to check out the places at the top of the list."

"Got it." He signed off and shook his head grimly. *Good luck.*

Right, Cam muttered to herself as she locked her car and joined the crowds on the ever-busy streets of Greenwich Village. *Time to play hide and seek.*

An hour later, she paid her third cover charge of the evening and thanked a leather-clad bouncer for a particularly garish skull and crossbones which she stamped on Cam's hand. Cam would never have known the boarded-up façade contained a club if she hadn't been given the address. The place was a warehouse on a dingy block just off Houston, its interior space divided into several levels. There were at least two bars that she could see, dance floors scattered at random, and what appeared to be a warren of smaller rooms in the rear. The massive area was dimly lit with recessed red lights, making it and its occupants resemble the scene of an accident.

The club was women-only and predominantly, but not exclusively, a leather bar. Cam bought a beer and began to wander through the crowded main room. Toward the rear, twisting halls led off to other much smaller rooms, all of them full. Scene rooms, she quickly ascertained as she caught glimpses of shadowy shapes engaged in various forms of sexual activity. Women in pairs leaned against walls, their hands inside each another's clothing, while others stood nearby, apparently watching. Here and there someone knelt, face pressed to the space between parted thighs. At one point she had to move sideways along the wall to pass two women clearly on the verge of consummating their encounter, oblivious to those pressing close to observe their heated exchange. She glanced into each of the smaller areas only long enough to note that Blair Powell was not among the participants. Why she found that a relief, she didn't know.

As soon as she pushed her way into yet another dark bar at the far end of the long hallway, Cam saw Blair Powell on the far side of the room. The first daughter leaned against the bar, one leg braced on the foot rail, facing in Cam's direction. Quickly, Cam turned her back and stepped behind a group of women who were congregated near the wall. She lifted her left wrist and whispered her location into the mike strapped there, issuing instructions to her agents concerning deployment of cars and ground positions. When Cam returned her attention to Blair Powell, the president's daughter had been joined by a heavily muscled blond in black leather pants and a sleeveless vest, who pressed close against Blair in the crowded space. The stranger appeared to be whispering urgently into Blair's ear, while Blair gazed past her into the seething crowd of bodies on the small dance floor, her expression remote, as if her mind were elsewhere.

The leather-clad woman was obviously trying to interest Blair in something a little more intimate than conversation, if her body language was any indication. She had stopped talking now and insinuated one leg on either side of Blair's thigh. The slow thrust of her hips was visible from across the room. Then she kissed Blair's neck and ran a hand up the inside of her blue-jeaned thigh. She would have pressed a palm to the triangle between Blair's legs if Blair hadn't gripped her wrist, pushing the hand away at the last second. Throughout the entire exchange, the first daughter was silent, her face barely registering a response.

It was clear to Cam that no one knew or cared who Blair was. Everyone was absorbed in their own pursuit of sex, or whatever particular thrill they were seeking. Still, Cam needed to be sure Blair remained anonymous, and she wasn't entirely sure how to do that. Calling attention to her by trying to remove her against her will certainly wasn't the best course of action. Plus, it was wrong. Despite the political ramifications, Blair Powell had every right to be there. Cam resigned herself to watching for the time being.

That proved to be more difficult than she had anticipated.

❖

"You'd better slow down, Tiger," Blair murmured. "You're melting my leg."

"Oh, man," the woman murmured hoarsely, her face close to Blair's ear. "You feel too good. You make me so hot…so fucking hot."

Blair edged away as much as the close space would allow, but her companion was not easily diverted. She trapped Blair against the bar with an arm on either side of her, riding Blair's leg harder, her motions jerky and tense. Blair turned her face away, avoiding an intended kiss. The woman's lips found her neck again instead, and a second later, she slipped one hand inside Blair's shirt. The fingers fondling her breast had no particular effect on Blair, but it apparently did on her ardent suitor. Her companion moaned shakily and shuddered, clearly poised to climax right there at the bar.

"Jesus, easy," Blair warned, caught off guard by the stranger's quick rise to orgasm. It hadn't been her intention to let the woman go that far, and she was about to cool her down when her eyes swept the room and met those of Cameron Roberts. Blair was momentarily stunned.

Her security chief leaned against the opposite wall, dressed in jeans, a white shirt, and boots. Her expression was completely impassive, and she looked completely at home. Roberts was also easily one of the sexiest women in the room and seeing her produced a jolt of excitement that even the woman about to come on her had not been able to elicit. The fact that Blair found the Secret Service agent attractive infuriated her, especially since she knew that the agent was only there to watch her. *Well, go ahead and watch.*

Keeping her eyes locked on Cam's, Blair cupped the stranger's buttocks in her palms, squeezing the taut muscles in small tight circles, lifting her leg hard into the other woman's crotch.

"Oh, fuck," the woman groaned, her entire body stiffening.

"Go ahead, baby," Blair whispered in her companion's ear. "You want to, don't you?"

"Oh, Jesus, yes," the stranger panted against her neck. "Oh, unhh—oh, I'm gonna come." She was so far gone all she sought was that elusive instant of bone-melting release. "Oh, yeah…"

Cam's gaze never strayed from the sexual display. Her face revealed no emotion, nor did Blair's, not even when Blair's partner in the drama shuddered into climax against her body. As the woman's spasms subsided, Blair extracted herself from her spent partner's embrace, grabbed her drink from the bar, and pushed her way into the crowd. She did not look back at the woman sagging against the counter, still gasping for breath, nor did she acknowledge the occasional appreciative comments her performance had elicited. She took her time crossing to Cam.

"Enjoy the show, Agent Roberts?" she asked as she stepped to Cam's side. The press of the crowds brought her within inches of her security chief. She could make out a light sheen of sweat on Cam's skin in the soft red glow of the lights. The urge to run a finger down the center of Cam's chest was more arousing than the sex Blair had already forgotten.

Cam's eyes were steady as she returned Blair's gaze. She might have been embarrassed to witness the encounter had she sensed a shred of intimacy in it. It was erotic, of that there was no doubt. She knew she was wet, but the physical arousal did not disturb her. It was purely reflex and barely registered in her consciousness. She hadn't been the only one watching, although the interest of the others was of a different nature. They had taken vicarious pleasure from watching Blair drive the other woman to her knees with need. That fact, the impersonal nature of it, bothered her more than anything. Blair Powell struck her as worthy of so much more. *But then that's not for me to decide, is it?*

"I have a car outside when you're ready to leave," was all Cam said. She had no intention of involving herself in Blair Powell's personal affairs, nor of commenting on them. She might have to *witness* them if Blair continued with this kind of public encounter, but she didn't have to be a participant.

"And if I decide to walk home?"

"As you wish," Cam replied. "I'll arrange for someone to accompany you."

"I'm not sure I've had enough entertainment just yet," Blair said pointedly. "She was a little too fast. The tough ones can never hold out long."

Cam shrugged, refusing to be drawn into a conversation about the sexual display she had observed. "The car will be outside no matter how late you stay."

"And where will you be?"

"Inside here with you."

"Watching?" Blair's voice held a trace of bitterness.

"Only as much as I have to," Cam replied softly, realizing as she said it how true the words were. She wanted to keep Blair safe, not watch her have sex with strangers.

Blair sipped her Manhattan, the only drink she'd had all evening. She might like to walk on the wild side, but she wasn't a fool. Studying Cam's face, she tried to gauge her attitude from her expression and found that she couldn't. The security chief leaned against the wall, completely relaxed, her tone friendly, her face composed. To anyone watching, they might be any two women in the first exploratory stages of a typical bar encounter. Except Blair knew they weren't, and as much as Agent Roberts made it appear that Blair had some choice in the rest of the evening, the truth was that the moment they had found her, her freedom had ended. She set her glass down hard on the nearest table.

"You don't make it as my choice for an escort, Commander," she said bitingly. "I'm going home."

Cam followed Blair out to the street at a discreet distance, and once she saw her climb into the car with two of her agents, she headed tiredly toward her own car. As she walked the few blocks in the dark, she tried not to replay the image of a strange woman surrendering to passion in Blair Powell's cold embrace.

CHAPTER FOUR

Mac was surprised to see the commander walk in at 0700 on Sunday. The report from the night watch said it was she who had picked up Egret's trail and tracked her down in the late hours of the night. Interestingly, there was no report on the surveillance inside the bar. Roberts would have to do that herself, and thus far she hadn't. He nodded hello as she poured coffee and joined him at the large central workstation.

"How long have you been on this detail, Mac?" she asked conversationally. She'd had three hours' sleep, and after rising, had worked out in the command center's gym for an hour. After showering in the agents' locker room, she'd dressed in the jeans and polo shirt she'd packed in her gym bag.

"Since the president's nomination," he replied.

"Is that true for the rest of the team?"

"Yes, ma'am."

"And have things been this out of hand the entire time?"

Mac held his breath for a second, trying to judge who he might potentially offend that mattered. He couldn't think of anyone. He expelled the breath almost gratefully. "Worse. At least last night we found her. There have been a half-dozen nights, and one whole weekend, when we didn't know where she was."

"Christ," Cam muttered. "How in hell did you keep that quiet?"

"Egret's not stupid." Mac grimaced at the understatement. "She knew we'd have to hit the panic button if she were *completely* out of contact, so she called in every few hours, randomly, from pay phones or her cell, to prove she was okay. We couldn't trace the calls, so we just ran around like assholes the whole time trying to find her."

"No repercussions?"

"Egret's got a lot of pull with her old man. If someone complains about her, and it gets back to him, it had better be serious or you're looking for a new job. And he doesn't seem to think a little joyriding is too serious."

"I do," Cam said flatly. "And since we're not going to get any help from above, we'll have to stay tight on her. But don't get in her way. She's most likely to run if we crowd her."

"I think everyone understands the plan."

"See that they do." Her voice was stone.

"Yes, ma'am."

❖

At 3:00 p.m., Blair emerged from her apartment building carrying her coat over one arm, nodded to the agent holding the door open for her, and climbed into the rear of the black Suburban waiting at the curb. Cameron Roberts was already inside. This was a pre-publicized event and the presence of the Secret Service was expected. The interior of the spacious vehicle was warm; the glass partition between the passenger area and the front seat where two other agents sat was closed.

"Good afternoon, Ms. Powell," Cam remarked as the SUV pulled into traffic. The first daughter had dressed for the gallery opening in a simple black dress, a single string of pearls at her throat. The thin straps accentuated the toned muscles of her shoulders and arms, while the scooped neck revealed just a hint of cleavage. The ensemble spoke of taste and understated elegance. It was hard for Cam to believe that the graceful woman seated across from her was the same one she had seen engaged in anonymous sex just hours before. But then the public persona was so often merely a façade. She knew that from experience.

"Agent Roberts, we meet again. Are you to be my date today?" Blair asked mildly. She noted that her security chief looked well attired for the semiformal gathering in a charcoal gray silk suit and monochromatic shirt, fashionably cut and beautifully tailored to her long, tight form. *This is one public servant who does not buy her clothes off the rack.*

"I was planning on coming inside after you made your entrance." The guest list was a mixture of every important art collector in the city, many of the noted artists, and a smattering of politicians. Cam had photos of everyone, and invitations would be required for admission to the Soho gallery. They had an advance team already in place doing routine crowd surveillance, and three agents would meet the car to escort Blair across the sidewalk. Despite the close security, this type of situation was the most dangerous for Blair—a public function, advertised in advance. At the very least, there would be curious onlookers gathered outside. Cam planned on being inside with two other agents, while the second team waited in the car. "It's not the best idea for me to be too easily identified...for those times we'd prefer *none* of us be recognized."

"Times like last night, you mean?" Blair's laugh was brittle. "When it might be *embarrassing?*"

"For those times when you might like as much privacy as possible," Cam amended quietly.

Blair stared at her. "You'd like me to think you care?"

Cam shrugged lightly, a small smile flickering at the corner of her mouth. "The happier you are, the happier I'm going to be."

Blair laughed again, this time with no restraint. "You are honest at least, although I'm not sure how far that will get you."

"It's the only card I have to play," Cam said seriously.

"Your approach is certainly novel, Commander." Blair surveyed her coolly. "I'm used to strong-armed tactics—'behave or else.' No one has tried the humble 'I'm just here to look after you' routine before. I suppose you think I'll fall for that and suddenly bare my...soul...for you?"

Her tone was mockingly suggestive, and her frank survey of Cam's body left little question of her intent. She shifted slightly on the leather seat, exposing an expanse of smooth, well-muscled thigh.

Cam smiled, unperturbed. No matter how attractive Blair Powell was, and she was damned attractive, Cam had no intention of being sidetracked. "If I can do my job without getting in your way, I will. As much as that is possible, I'll see that that happens.

There'll be times when it's impossible. I'll apologize in advance for that."

"But you won't bend the rules—not even as a favor?" Blair questioned softly, her tone heavy with innuendo. "I can be very generous with my repayment."

"No," Cam stated flatly. She bent her head slightly as a voice in her ear apprised her of their location. Looking up, she caught the surprise in Blair's eyes before her elegant features set into an expression of arrogant dismissal.

"We're almost there," Cam informed her. "One of the agents will walk you in."

"I know the drill," Blair snapped, irritated at the agent's implacable demeanor. *Maybe I'm wrong. Maybe Roberts is straight after all. But the way she looked in the bar last night! So damned hot. And she seemed so comfortable there.*

Knowing Cam was watching from across the room while the stranger in leather took pleasure from her body had been an incredible turn-on, more exciting for her than anything the woman had been doing. That realization had unsettled her, and she wanted Cam to feel as disquieted as she had been the night before. So far, she hadn't been able to crack her chief's cool exterior. If she couldn't unbalance Cam in some way, it was going to be very difficult to elude her and her watchdogs.

"Enjoy the opening, Ms. Powell," Cam said quietly as she slid from the vehicle and held the door for her. Blair did not grace her with a response.

❖

A willowy blond in a form-fitting navy silk sheath greeted Blair with an affectionate hug and whispered softly, "Hey, darlin'. I called you all last evening. Out on the prowl?"

Blair returned Diane Bleeker's hug, then shrugged imperceptibly, aware of the reporters nearby. "For a while."

They moved away from the crowd milling around the small bar where the obligatory wine and cheese was being offered. Blair smiled at the people she knew as well as those she didn't. She had so much practice at this, she barely registered the faces any longer.

"Get lucky?" Diane probed with the slightest edge in her voice. They had known each other for years, since prep school at Choate, where they had been lovers briefly. There had been more than one time since then that Diane wished they still were. There were moments when she caught sight of Blair unexpectedly, and her breath would catch with sudden desire. Blair was beautiful, talented, intelligent, and—most attractively—emotionally remote. Just the kind of challenge Diane liked in her women. When she looked at the cool, self-contained woman beside her, she barely remembered the eager, open young girl with whom she had first shared love and simple, unbridled sexual pleasure. She hadn't caught a glimpse of her in years.

"Depends on how you define lucky." Blair's smile was brittle. "*I* enjoyed *her.*"

"Did she enjoy *you?*" Diane pushed, knowing full well Blair rarely allowed her sexual conquests the pleasure of having her. Which was one of the reasons Diane remained attracted. Like the exquisite, one-of-a-kind works of art she brokered, Diane lusted after the exceptional, the singular, the one thing that no one else had. She wanted to be the one to wrest a cry of passion from those beautiful lips, to break the silence of Blair's isolation.

"She got what she was looking for." A warning flickered in Blair's blue eyes. There were places where even her oldest friend was not welcome. "She left satisfied."

Yes, but did you? Diane wisely decided to let it go. There was business at hand. She surveyed the room, pleased at the turnout. Whenever she showed Blair's paintings, there was interest. Some of it, of course, was due to Blair's notoriety, but most of it was due to her genuine talent. The collectors were beginning to buy her work, recognizing its value. It wasn't a solo showing this time, but Blair was the featured artist.

"Where's your new spooky?" Diane asked.

"Directly across the room. She just came in," Blair responded. Cameron Roberts was looking casually in their direction without seeming to focus on them. She was good. Blair knew perfectly well that *she* was the only thing her security chief was looking at. She also knew that the handsome agent saw her only as an assignment— an object to be moved, contained, and controlled on some giant chessboard. Blair might be the queen, but she had been stripped of her power. She was ruled by pawns, and she hated it. Especially when her keeper was a woman so attractive that she felt a twinge of desire every time she saw her. That made her even more eager to escape those intense gray eyes.

"Oh my," Diane murmured, following Blair's gaze. She took in the lean physique and androgynous features in one swift, appraising glance. "Now she *is* tantalizing."

Irked at the suggestive tone in Diane's voice and even more irritated at her own surge of possessiveness, Blair snapped, "Yeah, if she isn't being paid to watch you."

"*I'd* almost be willing to pay for that," Diane rejoined, ignoring the edge in Blair's tone. She had never let friendship stand in the way of her attraction to another woman, and if Blair was interested too, that just intensified the challenge. This one looked like she would take some work, though. There was a nearly visible barrier around her, her indifference shouting *look if you want to, I couldn't care less*. Diane loved bringing those untouchable types to their knees, so to speak.

"You need to mingle, darlin'," Diane said as she moved away. "And so do I if I'm going to sell anything."

Blair watched her seductively lithe friend melt into the throng, wondering how long it would take her to get around to Cameron Roberts. Frowning at the surge of concern, Blair turned with a smile to the director of the Museum of Modern Art, greeting him by name without a hint of her inner disquiet.

❖

"It's a shame you can't enjoy the artwork," Diane said softly as she moved next to Cam. "Not that watching Blair isn't enjoyable, of course." She extended one long-fingered hand. A diamond almost large enough to be ostentatious, but so beautiful as to be merely breathtaking, sparkled on her right ring finger. "I'm Diane Bleeker, Blair's agent."

"How do you do." Cam nodded politely, knowing full well exactly who the sophisticated woman beside her was, and intentionally not revealing her own name. "I *have* managed a glance or two at the works. You have a fine collection."

"See anything in particular that you like?" Diane queried teasingly. She didn't see the point in being coy. She was well beyond *that* point in her life. She allowed one leg to rest gently against Cam's trousered thigh. It could have been the press of the crowd that brought her so close, but they both knew it wasn't.

"Actually, yes." Cam registered the contact and the heat of Diane's leg against hers. She knew if she glanced down she would see the creamy expanse of the woman's breasts revealed by the low scoop of her softly clinging dress. She didn't look down. She gazed past her, instead, to where Blair stood in conversation with a young man who resembled every stereotype of struggling young artist she had ever seen—right down to the rumpled tweed jacket and scraggly beard. She kept her eyes on them as she spoke.

"There's a series of sketches, nudes, on the far right wall. Charcoal on paper. They're hers, aren't they?"

Diane studied her in surprise. She doubted many people had paid the small sketches much attention in the midst of the large oils and other canvases. But that wasn't the real reason for her careful answer.

"The artist is Sheila Blake."

"Uh-huh," Cam replied with a slight smile. "Ms. Blake's strokes resemble those of Ms. Powell, as does the use of light and shadow and spatial relationship. Of course, the president's daughter probably isn't interested in studies of female nudes. Are they for sale?"

"Yes," Diane replied, intrigued and immensely attracted.

"And the transactions are confidential?"

"If the buyer desires. Once the works are consigned to me, the buyer becomes my client."

"The buyer wishes to remain anonymous," Cam stated smoothly, shifting her position slightly to keep Blair in sight.

Diane caught her breath as Cam's arm unintentionally brushed her breast. She felt her nipple harden, painfully pleasant, and knew it was visible beneath the sheer material of her dress. *How is it possible to be this aroused by someone who is practically ignoring you?*

"I guarantee it," Diane managed, her voice husky.

"Thank you."

"Need we discuss price?" Diane asked, getting her hormones under control. She was a businesswoman, after all.

"That won't be necessary."

"Perhaps you'll allow me to take you to lunch then...to discuss the details." As she spoke, Diane rested her fingers on Cam's forearm, gently squeezing the hard muscles beneath the fine fabric.

Cam met her gaze fully for the first time, reading the invitation in them. "Lunch would be fine. I'll call."

"Yes, please do."

CHAPTER FIVE

When the phone rang, Blair was in the middle of a very interesting dream that had something to do with a dark-haired woman with extremely talented hands. Groaning, she groped for the portable phone, knowing she'd suffer from the unrequited erotic visions all morning.

"Blair Powell," she snapped.

"Are you awake?"

"Not yet, A. J.," Blair replied irritably as she slipped naked from the bed, the phone in one hand. "What time is it?"

"Time for me to be in a meeting. Talk to me now or wait until…God only knows when."

"Did you get what I need?"

"More or less. I don't think this is going to make you very happy."

Blair sighed as she pulled her robe around herself and stumbled toward the kitchen and her first cup of coffee. "Tell me."

"In a nutshell—she's not going to be easy to slip away from. Twelve years in the investigative division. Her specialty was tracking Colombian drugs paid for by counterfeit U.S. dollars. Crooks scamming crooks. Apparently she was very good at it."

Blair watched the coffee drip into the pot, her thoughts swiftly calculating. "Why is she suddenly assigned to protection? What aren't you telling me?"

"There are substantial holes in the intel on her. As a matter of record, she was involved in a multijurisdictional snafu earlier this year. The Secret Service had surveillance units watching a drug factory on the outskirts of D.C. Apparently the ATF was involved because they thought the same guys were trafficking guns in addition to the phony money. Unbeknownst to *either* federal agency, the D.C. narcotics unit had an agent undercover with the drug boys."

"Jesus," Blair muttered. "Sounds like a recipe for disaster."

"You got that right. Somehow the Colombians got wind that a bust was coming, and the narcotics detective's cover was blown. The bust went bad, and she was killed in a shoot-out. Cameron Roberts was shot trying to warn the undercover narc seconds before the whole place went crazy."

Blair's stomach tightened. "She was shot?"

"In the leg, apparently. That's not the whole story though."

"What is?"

"We're talking about one of the good guys here, Blair." Her caller hesitated. Even friendship had its limits. "Roberts has a sterling reputation."

"I don't intend to sully it," Blair snapped.

"There are rumors—not many, and no one will commit to knowing anything for sure. She's a hero, well liked by her colleagues—"

"All *right!* I get your point. You don't want to tell me, but you will. Because if you don't, I'll make sure you're *never* an assistant director."

"Blair!"

"I'm kidding, and you should know that, if you don't after all these years." Blair took a deep breath and got her temper under control. "Tell me who she is, A. J. She's got control over my life."

"Deep sources say the narcotics dick who was killed was her lover."

"Christ!" Blair breathed. That was not something she wanted to think too much about. She knew about loss, and she knew how long it hurt.

"That may explain the change in assignments," A. J. remarked. "A thing like that can ruin you for field work."

Blair pictured the clear-eyed, focused woman who had tracked her down at the bar with seeming ease two nights before. None of the other agents had ever been able to find her once she had slipped into the shadows. Or at least none had ever dared to.

"I don't think she's ruined for anything, A. J. She's ice."

"That would fit."

"What do you mean?"

"There's one other rumor, buried so deep I'm not even sure it's her they're talking about."

Blair sat on the edge of the stool at her breakfast bar, her coffee forgotten. "What is it?"

"You've heard of the very hush-hush escort service that operates on the Hill?"

"You mean the one that provides all kinds of companions— boys, girls, either or both—for senators, dignitaries, and supposedly, my father?"

"I don't know a thing about your father!"

"It doesn't matter one way or the other to me," Blair said wearily. "He leaves me alone, that's all I care about. What's this got to do with Roberts? Is she trying to shut it down?"

"Might be she's using it."

Blair caught her breath, then laughed derisively. "Your sources haven't seen Cameron Roberts. Believe me, A. J., she does *not* have to pay for sex."

"Maybe she wants to."

"Come again?"

"No strings, no attachment, nothing to lose."

"I forgot you're a psychologist," Blair commented dryly. She finally sipped her coffee. "So what you're telling me is that my new keeper has no weaknesses I might exploit to make a little breathing room for myself, huh?"

"None that I could find."

"Wonderful."

Blair gently replaced the receiver, her annoyance warring with her curiosity. *Everyone* had a secret, and everyone had a weakness—even her. She had just been lucky enough to keep hers hidden all her life. So, apparently, had Cameron Roberts.

❖

At precisely 11:00 a.m., a knock sounded at the door. Blair answered, knowing who it was.

"Always punctual, Commander?" she queried as she turned away, leaving Cam to follow her into the loft. As she walked, she caught back her wild blond hair with a headband fashioned from a black bandana. She pushed sweats and other gear that had been laid out on the couch into a nondescript gym bag, ignoring Cam as she packed.

"I thought we might go over the plans for the trip to D.C. and New Year's Eve," Cam suggested, leaning against the back of the couch.

"What's to review," Blair said dismissively. "You'll escort me to the airport, another hired guard will pick me up at National and deposit me at the White House. There I will play dutiful daughter, pose for a few photos, and celebrate surviving another year." She glanced at Cam with a shrug. "I'll tell you when—you be here."

"I would like to have the itinerary in advance so I can brief my team. Shall we plan on departure at 3:00 p.m. Wednesday?"

Blair finally faced her fully, her blue eyes flashing with irritation. "I am in the habit of setting my own schedule."

"That's why I'm here," Cam replied evenly.

"Do you spar, Agent Roberts?" Blair asked suddenly.

"As in hand-to-hand combat?"

"As in karate?"

Cam hesitated, momentarily at a loss as to where they were headed. Blair Powell did not make casual conversation. "Not exactly. I don't point spar; I'm a mat stylist. I—"

"Then let's talk about the travel arrangements after we work out. I was just leaving for the gym. You can use some of my gear."

Cam stared at her. This was not a good idea. She was paid to protect her, not socialize with her. She didn't care how it might look to others, but she was worried about maintaining professional distance. Blair was hard enough to handle without adding the confusion of any sort of personal relationship.

Stalling, Cam said, "If you're going out, I need to alert my people—"

"I'm outta here." Blair grabbed her bag, brushing past Cam. "You coming or not?"

Cam had no choice. She either went with her or allowed her to leave the building alone and hoped that one of her agents picked her up before Blair lost them in the crowds on the street. She hurried after her, activating her radio as she went.

"Mac, you there?" she whispered urgently.

"Yeah, boss," Mac answered immediately.

"Egret is flying. Get someone downstairs in a car."

"Roger that. You keeping her company?"

"Affirmative, but I want backup, and make sure everyone is mobile." She shouldered into the elevator just as the doors began to slide closed. Blair leaned against the rear wall watching her with an amused expression on her face. Cam clicked off the radio, clipped it back on her belt, and stared at her. She was more annoyed than angry, but she kept her expression neutral.

"You don't like it, do you?" Blair asked.

"Like what?" Cam asked evenly.

"Not being in control—not knowing what's going to happen one moment to the next."

"If we're speaking about my work, you're right. It's my job to be in the know, to have control of the situation. That's what I'm paid to do."

Blair studied her, unable to read anything in her smooth even features or her calm, modulated tones. The elevator doors opened into the foyer, and she saw two agents waiting near the door. She shook her head impatiently.

"Tell them to leave us alone," she said unexpectedly. There was a hint of something desperate in her voice.

"The gym on Seventh Ave?" Cam responded. *She's asking, not ordering.*

"Yes."

Cam spoke into her radio. "We're walking to Soho. Follow us in the car."

Cam and Blair stepped out into a brisk clear morning as the two men moved past them into the car that sat idling at the curb. It slowly drifted through traffic behind them as they turned south toward the gym.

"Are you really serious about protecting me?" Blair inquired of Cam, who walked beside her, constantly scanning the street ahead of them and the cars that passed alongside.

"Of course."

"Why?"

"Because you need it, and because I have been asked to do it."

"Would you actually take a bullet for me, as they say?" Blair asked mockingly.

"Yes," Cam answered curtly. A muscle clenched in her jaw, and a storm rose in her gray eyes. She locked eyes with Blair, searching for some hint of what she was after. She had no doubt there was a point to this. Blair's blue eyes were defiant, and just as searching.

"You've had some practice at that, haven't you?" Blair probed. Finally a swift intake of breath and a slight falter in Cam's step rewarded her as the question struck home. *She does have a weak spot,* she thought triumphantly.

When Cam failed to answer, Blair pushed. "It's a matter of record, you know."

"Then you know all there is to know," Cam replied stiffly, fighting to keep the image of Janet's face from her mind. She would not allow the memories to intrude here, not when she needed all her faculties to be sharp. What she needed to do now was the job. Just the job. Everything else was in the past—gone, over, dead.

"Really?"

"As you said," calmer now, "it's a matter of record."

Blair laughed. "We all know how accurate the records are, don't we, Agent Roberts?"

❖

Their destination was not the trendy urban health club where Blair practiced yoga and aerobics that Cam had anticipated. Blair led her swiftly past the expected entrance and turned down an adjacent alley. Cam groaned inwardly when Blair grabbed her arm and directed her up a flight of narrow, littered stairs in a run-down tenement building. They went through a double set of steel doors into a huge room on the third floor. It was a gym, of sorts.

The clientele was mostly male. Worn punching bags hung from chains attached to the rafters, and men in torn T-shirts or no shirts at all pounded at them. Heavily muscled lifters grunted and sweated at the free-weight benches tucked into every conceivable corner. Two elevated boxing rings dominated the center of the space, one currently occupied by a pair of fighters making a serious effort to score off each other. Cam was willing to bet there were half a dozen felons in the room, any one of whom probably knew exactly who Blair Powell was.

"Have you been here before?" she asked, trying to sound casual as she weaved her way around bodies, following Blair toward the rear of the long room.

"Three times a week for eighteen months."

Cam was furious. No one had told her about this place—she had no background on the members, no idea of the physical layout, and no prayer of guarding Blair effectively. How in hell had this been overlooked?

As if reading her mind, Blair commented, "They don't know about it."

"How?" Her voice was a growl.

Blair grinned, an altogether spontaneous and disarming grin. Or it might have been if Cam hadn't been so angry. "They think I'm at my massage therapist's office around the corner most of the time."

"Back door?"

"Uh-huh."

Cam didn't ask her why. There was no need to. She knew why. Pointing out the danger would be meaningless. Blair obviously cared less for her safety than for her freedom, and that was probably the result of having people like Cam constantly shadowing her for the last dozen or so years of her life. What mattered now was that something similar not happen again.

"Here we are," Blair announced airily, pulling back the curtain to a small, cramped dressing room not much bigger than a walk-in closet. A shower stall and toilet were visible behind a rickety screen in one corner. Blair tossed her bag down and in one fluid motion pulled off her shirt. The movement caught Cam off guard, and Blair laughed knowingly as Cam's eyes flickered once to her breasts before she quickly looked away.

"You can grab sweats and a T-shirt from my bag. There's plenty," Blair informed her as she continued to strip. She watched unabashedly as Cam changed. She knew Cam was aware of her scrutiny, although the agent gave no sign of it.

Her security chief had the kind of body Blair expected—lean and hard-muscled, a beautiful combination of female grace and power. She imagined making those muscles quiver with desire, watching the rigid control break with need. The force of the image stirred a flush of arousal so keen it made her gasp. If Cam heard, she gave no sign of it as she reached for a pair of sweats without hurrying.

Blair studied the ten-inch scar that ran down the outside of Cam's right thigh. It was still fresh enough that it hadn't lost the redness. As Cam pulled the pants up, Blair asked, "Is your leg okay?"

"Yes, it is."

Cam pulled on a T-shirt that said "Ernie's Gym," then faced Blair, who stood appraising her. The president's daughter wore a sleeveless tee, torn off a couple of inches below her high firm breasts, and baggy sweats. Sleek, well-toned muscles defined her arms and legs. Her exposed midriff was taut, and she sported a small gold ring in her navel. Untamed blond strands escaped from the black headband, wilding around her face. Her blue eyes glinted with brazen sensuality. She was a beautiful animal.

"I take it this is Ernie's?" Cam remarked dryly, refusing to be distracted by Blair's open seduction. The time when the promise of a body like that might have interested her was past. The price of possession was far too high.

"This is Ernie's," Blair rejoined, pushing the curtain aside. She wasn't perturbed by Cam's rebuff. She would have been disappointed had it been easy. What bothered her was the undeniable throbbing in her own body. Desire was a weakness, one she exploited in others but avoided personally. There were too many ways in which other people controlled her. She would not allow another.

❖

Cam's head snapped back as another kick landed along her jaw.

"Are you sure you don't want a helmet?" Blair called, a hint of laughter in her voice. She moved lightly on the canvas, her gloved hands at chest level. Cam faced her, wearing no gloves or other protective gear.

"No thanks," Cam responded, cautiously gauging the reach of Blair's legs with respect. When the next kick came she stepped off the line of its trajectory and deflected it with a forearm. She expected a follow-up punch, and she blocked that as well. She stepped back once again to a middle range, trying to get a feel for Blair's tactics. Blair moved lightly on the canvas, agile and supple. Blair was a kickboxer and used her feet as weapons in the ring. Cam, on the other hand, was trained for combat. She needed to be careful, because she had no desire to injure her.

Blair seemed to have no such concern, however. She attacked relentlessly, mixing kicks, double kicks, and punches with considerable skill. Some scored, and some would have done damage had they been full force. Cam deflected, blocked, and redirected her opponent's efforts. She was trained to immobilize and neutralize, and those techniques were not designed for sparring. She knew she couldn't defend this way for long. There was a good chance Blair would make serious contact with one of her kicks. As a sweeping roundhouse kick approached her head, Cam stepped forward into Blair's body, so close to her that the kick lost its force. She trapped Blair's leg with her near arm, grasped the shoulder of Blair's shirt with her other hand, and swept Blair's supporting leg out from under her. Cam held onto Blair to break her fall, followed her down to the mat, and pressed her face down with a shoulder pin.

"Son of a bitch!" Blair muttered as she struggled briefly to lift her torso off the canvas. She stopped when the pressure on her shoulder increased slightly. She wasn't damaged, but she was effectively immobilized.

"If you tap the mat, I'll release you," Cam said softly into her ear. "But you must promise not to punch me as you get up. Rules of war."

Blair laughed as she slapped the mat. She rolled over and found Cam kneeling beside her, a half smile on her face.

"You okay?" Cam asked.

"Dandy. I suppose you'll do that again if we start over?"

"I *told* you I didn't spar," Cam said as they both got to their feet. "I can't fight you on your terms. You'd annihilate me."

"No, I don't think so," Blair replied softly, stripping off her gloves. "You mind showing me that technique?"

Cam glanced outside the ring, only just realizing that they had drawn quite a crowd. Irritated that she had allowed her attention to be diverted from surveillance, she shook her head. She couldn't very well watch the people around them if she was flat on her back.

"This isn't a good time for a lesson. I don't even have anyone else inside the building."

Blair followed her gaze, her smile disappearing in annoyance. "They don't know me," she said flatly.

Cam saw the resentment in her eyes and shook her head slightly. "You can't know that."

"I know," Blair insisted. "I always know." She took a deep breath, then added in a whisper, "please."

Cam swept the group leaning on the ropes one more time. "All right."

She demonstrated at half-speed several times while Blair watched intently. Then she launched a kick toward Blair's head, ready to pull back if Blair failed to execute the technique. Blair quickly countered and took Cam down soundly to the cheers of the onlookers. Cam found herself on her back with Blair above her, Blair's bent forearm pressed to her neck. Blair wedged her knee between Cam's legs and leaned forward until their faces were nearly touching. Her lips were a breath away.

"If you don't slap the mat, I can make this feel a whole lot better," Blair whispered.

Cam gasped as Blair unexpectedly rocked her thigh hard into her crotch. For a second all she felt was the fire, igniting instantly into a consuming ache. She caught back a moan, shook her head to clear it, and in one upward hip thrust, dislodged Blair from on top of her. Cam jumped quickly to her feet, and in the next instant, vaulted over the ropes and out of the ring.

"She's too much for you, huh girl?" a burly man next to her said good-naturedly.

"You got that right," Cam responded lightly. She waited as Blair climbed down, then followed her into the dressing room.

"I need to shower," Blair informed her, pulling off her clothes.

"I'll wait outside." Cam said briskly, struggling to quell the remnants of unwanted desire.

"What are you afraid of, Agent Roberts?" Blair taunted lightly as she stood naked before her. "I *felt* you, you know."

"Take your time," Cam said evenly as she stepped out through the curtain. Blair's laughter followed her even as the throbbing in her pelvis reminded her of her own weakness.

❖

Cam slammed the conference door hard enough that the glass enclosure rattled. Six agents sat slumped around the table, staring at their pens. Cam stood at the end of the table, breathing heavily, trying unsuccessfully to contain her anger.

"How many of you have been on this detail longer than six months?" she asked at length, her words clipped. There was a moment of silence, then Mac cleared his throat.

"All of us, ma'am."

"All of you." She looked them over one at a time. "*All* of you."

"Yes, ma'am," he responded, his voice low.

"Obviously none of you are capable of this assignment, nor worthy of it. Blair Powell—the daughter of the president of the United States—has been criminally unprotected for *months*, and not one of you reported it? Even if I could overlook your lack of responsibility to her—which I can't—it is impossible to excuse your silence regarding the potential danger to national security. Were she kidnapped, it would threaten the presidency." Leaning forward, both hands flat on the table, she said succinctly, "I want a request for transfer from every one of you on my desk in one hour."

As Cam turned toward the door, Paula Stark stood abruptly. "Commander!"

"Yes?" Cam questioned sharply, looking back over her shoulder. The dark-haired, intense young agent was ramrod straight, her jaw set. *Determined. And not afraid.*

"I don't want a transfer, ma'am. I want this detail."

"Really? And why is that?"

Stark took a deep breath. "Because she's my responsibility, and because I can do what no one else can. I've spent the last few months following her through half the gay bars in this city. I'm recognized in those places, and I'm accepted by the clientele. I can go where most of the others on the team can't. You need an inside person, and, respectfully, that's me. Ma'am."

Cam regarded her silently. *Well put, Agent.*

"I know I should have filed a report sooner." Paula held Cam's penetrating gaze unflinchingly. "We lose her regularly, and it's always because we're never informed of her route, or she changes it, or she intentionally lies to us. We're all frustrated—but that's no excuse."

"You're right. There's no excuse for the dereliction of duty you've all been a party to. Regardless of Ms. Powell's duplicity, it is your sworn responsibility to guard her. If you don't have what it takes, you don't belong here." She looked over the group. "I don't want anyone on this team who doesn't want to be here. I'll see that there are no repercussions if you request transfer immediately, but I *guarantee* I will see you posted to an embassy in Somalia if you fuck up on my detail."

An hour later, Mac knocked on the door to Cam's unadorned eight-by-ten office.

"Commander?"

Cam studied his almost too handsome face. His blue eyes were serious.

"Are you staying or leaving, Mac?"

"I'm staying if you want me. Two men, Young and Johnson, want transfers—they're bringing the paperwork. I'm sorry I fucked up. If you don't trust me…"

Cam stopped him with a raised hand. "I need a good coordinator, Mac. We have an uncooperative subject, and nothing is going to change that. We are going to have to be able to readjust personnel, vehicle placement, even motor routes at a moment's notice. I need to be with her consistently and persistently until she figures out that we are not going away."

She saw the look of disbelief he quickly tried to hide. She laughed, the tension easing from her shoulders for the first time since she'd left the gym. "Yeah, I know. I'm dreaming. You'll be the desk jockey most of the time we're stationary, and the communication center when we're not. Are you in or not?"

He favored her with a brilliant smile. "I'm in."

"Good. Then find me replacements for the two who are leaving. I don't even want to see the files until you've been through them. And Mac—we both know what the problem has been." Her gaze was unwavering, and for an instant, rage flared in her dark eyes. "If there's even a hint of homophobia in anyone's record, I don't want them on this assignment. Blair Powell's sexuality is not our concern and shouldn't affect the way we do the job. I want that clear."

"Yes, ma'am. I understand." Inwardly, he felt a surge of satisfaction. *Finally, someone who is willing to face the issues and say what needs to be said.*

"Good. We'll brief for the trip to Washington at 0700."

As soon as her second in command closed the door, Cam leaned back in her chair and closed her eyes. She'd dealt with the problems with her team, now it was time to face her own dilemma. Blair Powell had gotten to her. *Jesus, in three days.*

She didn't want to think about her response to Blair's blatant sexual overture at the gym, but she had to. She could not afford to be distracted, and there was no denying the effect Blair had on her. The sight of her nude, the feel of her body, even the constant challenge of her intractable insistence on independence. All of it aroused her. Fortunately, it was purely physical, and they would be in Washington in two days. She could satisfy the unrelenting demands of her body then.

Chapter Six

Cam was the last one on the plane. The cabin space was small, and Blair sat alone in the back. Mac, Stark, and Ellen Grant, the other female agent, had boarded earlier and occupied the area just behind the cockpit. Cam nodded to them as she moved toward the rear, finally settling in the seat across the aisle from Blair. She stretched her legs into the aisle and pulled a stack of memos from her briefcase.

"Do you have plans for tonight, Agent Roberts?" Blair asked. She liked the semi-casual look of Cam's pressed khaki chinos and matching blazer over a blue broadcloth shirt. The only way she liked her better was in the tight faded jeans she wore when she was off duty. Blair remembered very well how good Cam looked in those. In fact, every time she thought about that night in the bar, she wanted nothing more than to get her hands inside those jeans. For the moment at least, that seemed unlikely. "A hot date, perhaps?"

Cam smiled, shaking her head slightly. "No plans. Happy birthday, by the way."

Blair flushed slightly, surprised at the personal remark. Most of the Secret Service agents made it a religion never to engage a protectee in anything other than a professional exchange. Then she reminded herself that the security chief was only being polite, like most of the people in her life. She leaned forward, lowering her voice as she spoke. "Why, thank you, Commander. I don't suppose a birthday kiss is in the offing?"

The soft sound of her voice was like a caress. Cam glanced at her, unable to ignore how attractive she was, then back at the papers before her. "No."

They did not speak for the rest of the flight.

When the Suburbans pulled up in front of the private entrance to the White House, Cam got out, held the door, and then accompanied Blair across the driveway. She stopped at the door as a guard opened it for Blair.

"I'll see you in the morning, Ms. Powell," she said. "Enjoy your day."

The door swung shut with no response from the president's daughter. The White House security staff would be responsible for Blair's welfare from this point until she was ready to leave the next day. Cam was looking forward to a day off, and, even more, to a relaxing evening. She waved off the car and walked away, punching in a familiar series of numbers as she left the White House, and Blair Powell, behind.

❖

A little after 9:00 p.m., Cam stretched out on the couch with a drink and watched the scene outside her living room windows. From her apartment she could see the glow of the White House in the distance. She wondered fleetingly how Blair was faring, then put the thought from her mind. Tonight she did not have to worry about her. She reached for the phone, checked to see that the scrambler was functional, and dialed.

"This is number 38913," she said as a female voice answered. "I'd like to confirm my arrangement for tonight." She waited for a moment as her client ID number was verified. "Yes, 11:00 at—" She hesitated as her beeper went off. "Just a second," she added, checking the number. It was the White House. "I'll have to call back. It may be later. Yes, keep it open; I'll take care of the additional time. Thank you."

She pushed the other line, keeping the scrambler engaged. "Roberts," she said tersely when the phone was picked up.

"Commander? It's Mac. I'm sorry to bother you, but I thought you'd want a call."

"Mac?" she said in surprise. "What are you doing there? What's going on?"

"I'm not supposed to be here. She's gone, Commander. They lost her an hour ago."

"God damn it," she cursed. "What do the ground teams report? What's the search status?"

There was a beat of silence. "Uh…they aren't looking, exactly. The team leader here didn't want anyone to know she'd…gone out…and decided to let her come in on her own. When it started getting late, a buddy of mine called me on the sly."

"She's out there loose? Are they nuts?" She took a breath, momentarily caught off guard by a swift surge of fear. Totally unlike her. In the next second, her mind was clear. "All right. Who else knows?"

"Just the inside team here. They haven't a clue where to look."

She understood his message. *They don't know she's a lesbian, and he doesn't want to tell them.* "Right—we can't very well call out our own people. We're not even supposed to know about this." She walked through to her bedroom, gathering her gun and keys as she went. "There are a few places I can check. Listen Mac, there's a floating club—it travels around from one venue to another all over the city. Very trendy, only people in the know have the address. Find it for me. I'll call you in an hour."

"How am I supposed to fi—"

She interrupted his protests. "I don't know how you'll do it, but I'm sure you will."

Two hours later, Mac finally had the address of the floating club. By then, Cam had been to every gay bar she knew of and several others Mac had come up with, and she was running out of ideas. It was almost midnight on New Year's Eve, and every bar was packed with exuberant men and women in various stages of intoxication and undress. She hadn't found her. For all she knew, Blair was tucked away in bed somewhere with a girlfriend they didn't know about. She hoped so.

When she convinced the bouncer to let her in to the exclusive party by offering a fifty in lieu of an invitation, it was worse inside than she expected. Loud music and wall-to-wall people, all of them jostling to find partners for the night. Smoke hung in clouds below murky spotlights. The air was heavy with sex and booze. She pushed her way into the shadowy depths of the room, hoping that each blond she saw would be Blair.

From across the room, the president's daughter saw Cam walk in almost immediately. For the last half-hour, Blair had been leaning against the wall just inside the hallway that led to the bathrooms, watching a young, tough number in tight black leather pants swagger about at the bar, apparently trying to impress her friends with her bravado. Blair thought she might be fun to toy with. It was always so satisfying to humble the butches, and she made a bet with herself that she could make this one beg inside of fifteen minutes. She was about to go over when she'd caught sight of Cam.

Taller by a head than most of the women, Cameron Roberts cut a swath through the crowd like a sleek cutter through the sea. In a light windbreaker, dark polo shirt, and the signature faded jeans and boots, she should have looked ordinary, but she was easily the sexiest woman in view. Graceful and certain, lithe and powerful, she was a hunter searching its prey. It was only the darkness in the hall that gave Blair the advantage. As Cam moved closer, Blair's pulse quickened. This time the hunted would have the hunter.

Cam stepped through the archway into the hall just as the countdown to midnight began. People were crushing in around her, searching for that elusive someone to claim at the dawn of a new year. Out of nowhere, Blair caught her by the arm and spun her against the wall, pressing hard along the length of her body.

Cam was momentarily stunned. She felt the softness of breasts against her chest, warm breath on her neck, a muscled thigh fitted tightly into her crotch. The assault of sensation was so unexpected she didn't have time to control it. Her breath caught as a stab of desire streaked down her spine and exploded between her thighs. Her clitoris swelled painfully, hard and ready in an instant. "Jesus, sto—"

"Happy New Year, Commander," Blair breathed into her ear as she grasped Cam's head and pulled her down into a possessive kiss.

"Unh," Cam moaned as Blair's searching tongue invaded her mouth, adding fuel to the fire that raged through her. Cam kissed her back; she couldn't help it. For an instant, she forgot where she was, or *who* she was. All she knew was the pounding in her head and the exquisite ache in her depths as she roared toward orgasm. Unconsciously, her hands came to Blair's breasts; Blair gasped and pushed a hand between Cam's legs.

"Oh, Christ!" Cam groaned, pulling her mouth away so abruptly her head banged against the wall. Legs trembling, barely able to think, she jerked her hands from Blair's body as if burned. Blair's fingers were massaging her, pushing her so close. She grabbed Blair's wrist and dragged the hand away from her body. "No, God damn it! That's enough!"

"Are you crazy?" Blair exclaimed, her voice thick with arousal. "You're so hot, so *hard*, I can feel you through your jeans. You're almost there—let me do what I know you want."

"It's *not* what I want." That simple truth was all Cam needed to find her control. She pushed Blair back a step, breaking their contact. "I want to get you out of here."

Blair's eyes blazed dangerously at the knowledge that she had come close to humiliating herself. The fire in Cam's body had ignited her own, and she had been very close to coming herself. She throbbed still; the barest touch would send her over. *No one* did that to her, not unless she wanted them to. "Go fuck yourself, Agent Roberts!"

As Blair tried to walk away, Cam grasped her arm. "Ms. Powell, please."

"Leave me alone." Roughly, Blair shook off the restraining hand. "No one knows I'm here."

"*I* know."

"Then pretend you *don't*," Blair snapped, trying to escape into the crowd. She couldn't move very quickly through the mass of revelers, and Cam stayed right beside her.

"I can't," Cam stated with finality. She risked touching her again and slid her fingers around Blair's forearm, slowing her down a little. "Please."

Blair turned around, her body rigid with fury. "Then do your job, but stay out of my way."

"Fine. All right." Cam accepted the slight concession; she had no other choice. As much as she hated to do it, she let Blair move ahead of her. She wanted to call Mac for backup, but she was afraid if she took her eyes off Blair for a second, she'd lose her. The best she could do was stay close to her until she settled for the night, and then send for another team.

Despite Blair's efforts to leave her behind, Cam was still close enough to hear when the president's daughter walked up to a young woman with spiked blond hair, a tattoo on the side of her neck, and leather pants so tight they telegraphed that she had packed for action. By way of a greeting, Blair kissed her hard on the mouth and then announced, "I'm leaving. You coming with me?"

It took the stunned stranger a moment to find her voice, but when she did, she grinned cockily and said, "Name the place."

"Follow me, baby." Blair took her hand and dragged her toward the door.

Keeping a discreet distance, Cam followed them as they walked, arms wrapped around each other's waists. Every time Blair stopped to grope and fondle her leather-clad conquest, Cam stepped into the shadows. Blair never looked in Cam's direction, but she had to know Cam was there, watching the display.

If the seduction was meant to anger Cam, it did, but probably not for the reasons Blair intended. Cam was infuriated at the risk Blair was taking, picking up a stranger and then practically making love to her on the street a few blocks from the White House. It was dangerous on more levels than she could count. Blair Powell was beautiful, bright, and talented. She didn't need to waste herself on one-night stands. It was physically hazardous, politically suicidal, and willfully self-destructive. *And none of your business.*

When the young woman suddenly backed Blair against a wall and pushed both hands under her sweater, Cam came close to breaking up their little tryst. The sight of Blair pinned, nearly helpless, made her stomach clench. Swearing under her breath, Cam balled her hands at her sides and forcibly reminded herself that Blair Powell had every right to do what she was doing, and that any effort to intervene would only make her more reckless the next time. A second later, she heard Blair laugh and saw her push the amorous suitor away. A block further on, they disappeared into a hotel. Cam observed Blair book a room, then lead her new girlfriend to the elevators. As the door to the car slid closed, Blair fisted her hand in the woman's hair and kissed her.

Cam's blood was raging when she walked to the registration desk and slapped her ID onto the counter. "Give me that room number."

"But—"

"Do it and I'm gone. Make me wait *one* goddamned second, and I'll close this place down for the next six hours."

Two minutes later, at just after 1:00 a.m., she was on the phone in the lobby of the Franklin Hotel. Her call was answered immediately. "Mac?"

"Yeah, Commander. Tell me you got her—please."

"Send two of our people, not the White House detail, to the Franklin Hotel on the parkway. I'll wait until they get here. She's in Room 1302, and I think she'll be here for the night. I need someone in the room across from hers—I've booked it—and a car downstairs to intercept her when she leaves."

"Roger."

She rubbed her eyes, grateful that the hotel clerk hadn't paid much attention when Blair had signed in. Cam hadn't given him more than a glimpse of her ID, and she didn't think he'd recognized Blair. She shook herself, realizing that her mind was wandering. *Christ.* "And Mac, keep this quiet, for God's sake. If the White House press corps catches on to her little foray, they'll be all over us in the morning."

"Any info on who she's with?" Mac asked hesitantly.

"No," Cam said curtly. *Except whoever she is, we'd better hope she doesn't figure out who just picked her up.* She saw them again, Blair's mouth on the woman's neck, her hands traveling the length of her body. For just an instant, she felt Blair's breasts in her own palms and remembered fingers between her thighs, tormenting her with just the perfect pressure—

"Commander, you still there?"

"Yes," she retorted, her voice thick with the memory.

"I'll have someone there in five minutes," Mac repeated.

"Good." Cam drew a ragged breath. "Tell them to step on it."

❖

Cam was still seething with a dangerous combination of anger and arousal when she stepped off the elevator into the small foyer in front of her apartment. She stopped in surprise when she saw the stately blond seated on a bench in the alcove. Claire put a book aside and smiled in her direction.

"My god!" Cam exclaimed. "I didn't mean for you to wait out here in the hallway."

Her visitor stood, sliding the book into a stylish leather bag. "I know, but my evening was already planned, and it's safe enough. I know I'm presuming, and I can leave if you like. But you *did* book the whole night."

"No, come in," Cam said as she unlocked her door. "I still owe you a drink."

Cam hit the dimmer switch inside the door, giving them just enough light to maneuver by. She turned to the woman who stepped inside after her. "I'm sorry—"

"Don't be," the blond said, touching Cam's cheek briefly. When she lightly brushed her hand down Cam's chest, she heard the sharp intake of breath. She felt the tremor and the heat, too. She knew the signs. In a throaty whisper, she said, "You need some attention."

Without waiting for an answer, she pushed Cam gently back against the door and held her there with a palm against Cam's chest. With the other hand, she reached down to work loose the buttons on Cam's fly. The quick jerk of hips beneath her fingers was wordless assent. Moving her hand from Cam's chest to rest her arm along the wall, she leaned close and reached into Cam's jeans.

"Oh God," Cam groaned, praying she could stay standing. She was so hard it hurt, had been since Blair had touched her in the bar, and the urgent need had never quieted. The first touch was excruciating. She grasped the door handle for support and closed her eyes.

The strokes were certain, commanding and relentless. Cam heard herself moaning. Back against the wall, body rigid with the effort to control the mounting pressure, her hips bucked forward into the waiting palm. When fingers slowly pressed the length of her, she gasped, "I'm losing it."

"It's all right," a gentle voice murmured.

Clenching her jaw until it ached, she tried to hold on. Another firm caress and she broke. She shouted hoarsely as the explosion rocketed through her, her head rolling from side to side with each pulsation. When it finally subsided, she was amazed she was still upright.

"Oh, Christ," she panted breathlessly. "I didn't mean for that to happen so fast."

"I don't think it was up to you," her companion laughed softly, moving away discreetly so Cam could regain her composure. Claire knew that the arousal certainly had nothing to do with her, which she suspected was most often the case.

"Will you have that drink now?" Cam asked dryly as she fumbled with the buttons on her jeans. Her hands were trembling badly.

"I would definitely like that," Claire said with a smile. Inclining her head toward the bathroom, she added, "I'll be right back."

Cam moved over to the bar on still-unsteady legs and poured them each a drink. A minute later, they settled side by side on the sofa in front of the floor-to-ceiling windows. They sat in silence in the near-darkness for a few moments, before Cam asked, "Does it bother you? The lack of reciprocation?"

When her guest failed to answer, she added quietly, "I'm sorry. That was inappropriate, and none of my business."

"No, it's all right," came the soft reply. "I don't expect any reciprocation, and most of the time, I wouldn't want it."

Most of the time. It was Cam's turn to be quiet. As many times as they had met, they had never talked of anything personal. She had never wanted to know anything about Claire before. *Claire.* She'd never even wanted to know her name. She had no idea why she was asking now.

"This is a job, and you should understand that it is my choice to do this. There is absolutely no coercion involved," Claire added.

Cam believed her. Operations of this caliber were by referral only, and Cam had gotten hers from a very high ranking member of the Italian consulate. A diplomat she had known all her life had assured her that the service was safe and discreet, and that the escorts were extremely well paid. What Cam didn't know was who they were, or what they felt. Until their last meeting, both of them had kept their identities, and their secrets, hidden. It was a business arrangement with a veneer of civility, nothing more.

"So sometimes you would like it to go both ways?" Cam asked.

"I certainly wouldn't throw *you* out of bed," Claire replied gently, her laughter making light of her statement. "If that would please you."

"I'm not asking for that." Cam struggled with the words. How to explain that she hadn't felt any desire to touch a woman for months, that the thought of wanting someone terrified her, that it was too much, too close. That when the memories and the guilt made it impossible for her to think or sleep, sex would give her a few hours' peace, as long as she didn't feel anything except the rush of release. "I can't...I haven't—"

Claire stopped her with a hand on Cam's thigh. "I don't *need* you to make love to me. If it makes you feel any better, I enjoy what we do. Rather a lot. Exactly as it is."

Cam nodded in acceptance, because she was too tired and too shaken by her loss of control, first in the bar and then here, to think clearly. Placing her drink beside her on the table, she stood and reached out her hand.

"I want you to stay here tonight," she said, hoping eventually to sleep.

CHAPTER SEVEN

The next morning, Blair emerged from her room alone a little before 7:00 a.m. She said nothing as the two Secret Service agents came out of the room opposite her and fell into step by her side. Once in the vehicle, Blair leaned back and closed her eyes. She'd heard the team leader call Cam and inform her of their ETA at the residence. *Wonderful. I really want to see her right now.*

Cam was waiting at the side entrance of the White House when the Suburban pulled in. She watched Blair step out, looking faintly hollow-eyed and unusually strained. They had to hurry to get her past the press corps without announcing she had been out all night. And Blair looked *exactly* like she had been out all night, and up all night screwing. Cam figured she didn't look all that much better than Blair, because she felt like hell. Neither of them acknowledged the other. Cam ushered Blair in through the service entrance and down the labyrinth of halls to the elevator to the family living quarters.

"I'll be outside with the cars. The plane leaves at 0830."

"Fine."

The ride to the airport less than thirty minutes later had been just as frosty.

Once aboard, Blair stalked down the aisle and threw herself across the seats at the rear. Cam took the first seat inside the cabin, leaned back, and closed her eyes. She hadn't gotten much sleep. None of them had. Between tracking Blair down, then shadowing the hotel the rest of the night, half the team had worked on the one night they all expected to have off. When the plane landed in New York forty minutes later, Cam escorted Blair to the waiting SUV and climbed into the back with her. In an hour, Blair was due to meet with the mayor to emcee the New Year's Day parade.

"Where to, Ms. Powell?" Cam asked perfunctorily. Since Blair's disappearance the night before and her late arrival that morning, their entire schedule had been changed. Cam had no idea of Blair's plans and being at such a disadvantage infuriated her.

For once Blair appeared subdued. "I need to go home and change."

Cam nodded, passed the message along to the driver and the car following them, and settled back against the seat. She clamped down on her anger. She wouldn't give Blair the satisfaction of knowing how unsettling the interlude in the bar had been for her. The hours she had spent with Claire had satisfied her body, but they had not erased the memory of Blair's mouth on hers or the demanding promise of Blair's hands claiming her. It was not a memory Cam welcomed, and the faint bruises around Blair's lips only served to remind her that Blair had been up all night satisfying *her* needs with a stranger.

Christ, Roberts, don't be a fool. Anyone will do, as long as she's in charge. You just happened to be handy.

❖

When they pulled up in front of Blair's apartment, Cam sent Mac for coffee while she waited in the vehicle. She closed her eyes and thought of nothing. When the door opened again, she looked up and then quickly averted her eyes as Blair Powell slid into the rear seat and settled across from her. *This* woman looked nothing like the woman Cam had followed into a Washington gay bar the night before. That woman had been wild, untamed and untameable. Blair was a predator, all the more deadly because she was irresistible. She was beautiful in the way of wild animals, and Cam had fallen prey to her power even as she tried to deny it.

This woman was elegant and refined and bore no resemblance to the creature she had been the night before—the one exception being that she was just as unapproachable. The ferocious hunger in Blair's eyes had been replaced by a glacial stillness. If there were thoughts behind the ice blue wall, they no longer showed. Her tailored coat was open to expose a fitted suit, the jacket unbuttoned to reveal a silk camisole beneath. The skirt slid up as she crossed her legs. Cam found her every bit as attractive in this guise as she had been the previous night. Neither did she feel any safer, all too aware of the pounding of her own heart.

In defense, Cam forced herself to focus on the job at hand. This was one of the most dangerous kinds of appearances for Blair, since she would be exposed and highly visible in the midst of a large crowd. When they arrived at the central viewing area, where the mayor and Blair would be commenting on the passing parade, Cam was greeted by the mayor's chief of security, a serious-looking redhead in her early forties.

"Captain Landers," the redhead announced briskly, extending her hand while openly appraising Cam.

Cam nodded in response as she returned the firm grip. "Cameron Roberts."

Looking past her opposite number, Cam surveyed the podium where Blair would be seated. She frowned slightly, noting that the rear of the elevated platform was open where the trucks and vans carrying sound equipment and other video paraphernalia were parked. Anyone could approach from that direction, and she motioned for Mac to station several of their people behind the stand. Landers noted the maneuver, and quickly dispatched two of her own staff to join the Secret Service agents.

Blair watched in amusement as the two security chiefs surreptitiously checked each other out, the way two dogs would while surveying common territory. She was pretty sure that Stacy Landers was a lesbian, and from the way Landers had looked at Cameron Roberts, Blair was even more convinced. For a brief instant, she felt a flare of jealousy. There was no doubt that Roberts was one of the most arresting women she had ever seen, and she didn't doubt that there were plenty of women looking for her attention. The fact that it bothered her even for a second irritated her enormously. Blair turned her back on their activities, focusing on the mayor and his entourage. She certainly had no intention of allowing Cameron Roberts to occupy any more of her thoughts than necessary.

While she offered casual responses to the mayor's convivial chatter, Blair tried not to think about the previous night, or the fact that each time she had wrung a cry from her willing conquest, she had wished it was Cam responding to her caresses. She had been keenly aware that the body writhing beneath her was not the woman she had held for just a fleeting instant in the bar. Nor could she forget what touching Cam had done to her.

The desire that radiated from Cam's body then had been breathtaking. That lightning response had excited Blair so much that the lingering effects had carried her to a climax as she'd made love to the young stranger. She'd never undressed, never let herself be touched, but she'd come anyway, thinking of Cam. Even now, she couldn't put it from her mind. Cam's swift intake of breath, the sharp lift of her hips into Blair's palm—all of it had ignited Blair's passion in a way that no one had been able to do in longer than she could remember. Even thinking of it now stirred her anew. *Jesus, let it go. She won't give in. She's all about the rules and regulations.*

"Are you ready, Ms. Powell?" the mayor's aid inquired politely, prompting an automatic smile from Blair.

"Yes, of course."

Fortunately, she could do this sort of event without conscious thought. She had been in the limelight since adolescence. She smiled at the appropriate times, she made the appropriate complimentary remarks about the performers, and she was altogether gracious and charming. To make things even easier, the camera loved her. In any lighting, her face looked as if it had been sculpted on a Grecian coin. Because of her personality and her appearance, she was frequently asked to preside at such media events. She did it because she had to, and because she cared about her father's image.

Nevertheless, each appearance took its toll. She was aware of men around her staring with thinly veiled looks of barely disguised lust. She would not have tolerated it under any other circumstance. Had it happened on the street, where she was not as immediately recognizable, she would have made it very clear she was not interested. As it was, she had become an unwilling participant in the charade. She had never quite gotten used to it, and the subterfuge demeaned her in her own eyes and heightened her anger. Only at night, when she shed her public persona and grasped what little she could of her own life, did she feel genuine.

For some strange reason, that afternoon she was acutely aware of Cameron Roberts standing just behind her out of the line of sight of the camera. The knowledge that Cam knew the truth about her somehow made the entire event more bearable—her presence reminded Blair of whom she really was. When the event was over, she thanked everyone and turned wearily away. Cam was instantly at her side.

"Ready to go?" Her tone was gentle. Blair's exhaustion was evident.

"God, yes."

Blair didn't relax until they were in the Suburban again on their way back to her apartment. Cam sat across from her in silence. However, it was not the heavy awkward silence of the earlier ride from the airport, but rather a comfortable regathering of energy after the stress of the afternoon. Blair had to admit that she had felt safe. Despite all the years of these kinds of experiences, she had never quite gotten over the feeling of being vulnerable. There was something about Cameron Roberts's presence that allowed her to forget for the moment that millions of eyes were upon her. It wasn't that the dozens of others who had preceded Roberts hadn't taken their job seriously, but Blair had always known it was the job and not her they were working for. What made Cam so compelling, and at the same time so irritating, was that when she focused on you, you knew you had been seen.

"Thank you for handling that so well," Blair said.

"You're welcome."

"Come upstairs, Commander," Blair said as the vehicle glided to a stop in front of the brownstone. "We can go over the schedule for the rest of the week."

Cam quickly hid her surprise at the unusual invitation. "Certainly."

When the rear doors opened, Cam stepped out first. She glanced quickly up and down the street, ascertained that the area was secure, and extended her hand to Blair. It was an automatic gesture, and she did it without thought.

Blair hesitated for just a second and then took the offered hand. The grip was firm and cool. She ignored the tingling in her fingers. "Thank you."

The other members of the team escorted them to the private elevator that went only to Blair's penthouse, then left to take the second elevator to the control room just below it. As the elevator doors opened on the uppermost floor, Cam exited and, out of long habit, visually swept the hall. In one swift movement, her gun was drawn. Abruptly, she turned toward Blair, who had stepped up beside her, and grasped her around the waist. She pushed Blair forcefully back into the elevator, shielding her from the foyer with her own body.

"Stay behind me," she ordered as she slapped the lobby button. "Mac," she said urgently into her microphone. "Seal the building. Have team one meet us at the elevator. We have code red."

"What's going on?" Blair demanded anxiously.

"We're evacuating." Cam held up one hand to silence her, still speaking to her second in command. "There's a package outside Egret's apartment door. Call the bomb squad."

The elevator door slid open and four other agents quickly surrounded them. Cam led the way, walking directly in front of Blair to block her body from any possible sightline. The group hustled the startled woman across the lobby, through the double glass doors, and into a waiting vehicle. Within seconds the Suburban was speeding through the late New Year's Day traffic.

"Clear the civilians from the building," Cam said as she listened on her radio to what was happening in the command room. "Keep them all together for questioning. I want a list of every person who was in the building within the last week. Right…I'll advise you when we reach the safe house."

"What?" Blair demanded. "Where are we going?"

"Temporary quarters," Cam responded.

"For how long?"

"Until I can assess the degree of threat."

The safe house turned out to be a large suite on the top floor of one of the exclusive hotels uptown. As soon as they entered, Cam was in communication with Mac once again. Meanwhile, Blair was left to pace in silence in the sitting room. The instant Cam ended the call, Blair confronted her.

"Do you mind telling me what the hell is going on?"

"Someone left you a present. Until we find out what, and who, you are not safe at home."

"And I suppose you think I'm going to stay here?" Blair asked, incredulous.

"I don't have time to argue with you. Your safety, not your comfort, is what matters at the moment. Once I have some idea of what was in the box, and how someone was able to gain access to the penthouse without our surveillance cameras picking them up, I can give you some idea of when you can return. The entire security system will need to be revamped, and your apartment needs to be swept."

"What about my work?" Blair asked intently. She couldn't quite keep the tremor from her voice. "All of my work is in my loft. It's protected from fire, but not from a horde of careless Secret Service agents tramping through my apartment."

Cam recalled the stacks of canvases and works in progress that filled over half of Blair's loft space. The artwork was irreplaceable, and quite possibly priceless. What she saw in Blair's eyes, however, was not concern for the material loss, but for the loss of her creations. For an artist to lose her work was the equivalent of anyone else losing a body part.

"I understand," Cam said immediately. "I'll talk to Mac and make sure that everyone is aware of what's in your apartment. We have to look at everything. There could be almost anything hidden almost anywhere. If someone was able to penetrate our security to leave a package outside your door, we have to assume they had access to the interior of your apartment as well. I'm sorry. It's the best I can do."

Blair searched Cam's eyes and found sincerity as well as empathy in the depths of her dark gray eyes. "Thank you," she whispered softly.

"As soon as we have things under control, I'll have someone bring your clothes. Is there anything else you want?"

"A different face?" Blair grimaced. "Can you have someone bring me one day of anonymity?"

"How about pizza and a six-pack of Corona?"

Blair laughed in spite of herself. "If that's the best you can do, Commander, you are one lousy date. However, considering the limited resources at hand, I'll take it."

❖

As it turned out, it was six hours before Cam was satisfied that there was no immediate danger at the apartment building. The package wrapped in plain brown paper that had been left in front of Blair's door did not contain a bomb. The dogs sent in to investigate were completely uninterested, and there wasn't anything to excite them in Blair's apartment either. A half-dozen agents had scoured the loft and found no evidence of tampering.

Mac was on his way over with the package and supplies for a few days' stay. Cam estimated it would take that long to change all of the locks on the building, recheck all the security clearances of the cleaning crews, maintenance men, and inhabitants of the other apartments, and review all of the transient visitors to the building for the last week. She hadn't told Blair of the timetable yet and wasn't looking forward to doing it. Until they had a better idea of exactly what had happened, she couldn't let Blair leave the safe house.

Cam intended to stay on site personally for at least the next several days. Mac was already arranging around-the-clock coverage at the hotel. The suite had two bedrooms, a large sitting area, a bar, and wide-screen TV. They would be cramped, but they would all have to manage.

A knock at the door brought her to attention. She crossed the width of the room quickly, reaching into her jacket to release the snap on her shoulder holster as she moved. She relaxed as Mac announced his arrival.

"What have you got for me?" she asked immediately.

Mac hefted a shoebox-sized parcel in his hands. "I've got this. Bomb boys and evidence techs are done with it."

"Excellent." She indicated that he join her at the table in the sitting area. Blair appeared at the door of the master bedroom just as Cam was reaching for the parcel. Their eyes met, and Cam read the question that Blair could not bring herself to ask.

"Join us, Ms. Powell, please," Cam said quietly. At Mac's quick expression of surprise, she merely regarded him steadily. She need give no explanation. It was her call to make.

Once Blair took the seat to Cam's right at the small table, Cam carefully examined the exterior of the package. The only address was Blair's name written in block letters with black magic marker. No postal stamp or other identifying marks. The wrapper appeared to be ordinary packing paper sealed with Scotch tape. Carefully, Cam lifted the tape and removed the paper to reveal a cardboard box. A slight residue of fingerprint powder adhered to everything, inside and out. She unfolded the flaps and removed a single sheet of paper. She looked at it for a second, then placed it flat on the tabletop so Blair and Mac could read the words printed there. A muscle in her jaw bunched tightly as she reread the hand-printed words.

You are so beautiful.
Why do you waste yourself on those who are not worthy?
I know how rare and precious you are.
I can forgive your sins.
I am watching.
I am waiting for your sign.

"Oh, Christ," Blair breathed. She suddenly felt cold, as if a strange hand had run over her naked flesh. Unconsciously, she leaned closer to Cam.

"Have Grant return this to the lab for handwriting analysis and get me a readout on the paper," Cam instructed, her voice stone. *You son of a bitch. You will never get this close to her again.*

"Roger," Mac replied quietly.

"I want twenty-four-hour a day real-time photo surveillance of the street in front of the apartment building. Assign our best tech person to it. I want to see any repeaters, any loiterers, and anyone who seems the slightest bit out of place." Cam kept her hands flat on the table, because she had the overwhelming desire to punch something. Just hours ago, Blair had been exposed to the view of thousands. The night before, she'd been wandering the streets of D.C. with a stranger. From all reports, she'd been vulnerable for weeks. *And we've been sitting around doing nothing to protect her. Well, that's over now.*

"It's a stalker, isn't it?" Blair questioned, hoping there might be another answer.

"I'm afraid so," Cam responded. This was the worst possible news. Stalkers were unpredictable and difficult to identify, and frequently did not have a previous police record. Everywhere Blair Powell went, she would be in potential danger. Cam's job had just gotten ten times harder, and considering the difficulties they already had in keeping track of a reluctant subject, the work ahead looked dismal.

"When can I go home?" Blair asked quietly.

"It will be at least a week," Cam replied honestly.

"You've got to be kidding!"

Cam laughed humorlessly. "I really wish I were."

"Should I get the chief of staff on the line, Commander?" Mac questioned.

"I'm getting to it." Cam sighed. "I just wanted to go over the tapes from the video cameras first. Have you got them?"

"Please don't bring in Washburn," Blair said urgently.

"I have to. You must know that," Cam responded.

"Can't you wait? If you inform the White House, this will be all over the news tomorrow. I'll never have another moment's peace."

Cam looked at her across the table. There was something close to pleading in her eyes.

"Could you give us a minute here," Cam said to Mac.

Mac looked as if he wanted to protest, but after a second he stepped out into the hall.

Cam leaned toward Blair and said gently, "This is serious. I can't keep something like this from my superiors."

"Don't tell me you're worried about being reprimanded." Blair laughed in disbelief.

"That's not the issue. If this escalates, I may need more help. I'm not willing to jeopardize your safety to protect your privacy."

"We're not talking about my *privacy*." Blair's voice rose, and she made an effort to control it. "We're talking about my private *life*, and that's what I don't want on the six o'clock news."

"Is it really the news you're worried about?"

"Perhaps it isn't. But in the end, it's all the same." Blair briefly touched Cam's hand, surprising them both. "There's not much difference being between stalked by an overzealous admirer or by a horde of hungry reporters. Either way, I'm the victim."

Cam shook her head, ignoring the surge of empathy. Ignoring, too, the lingering heat of Blair's fingers on her skin. "Even if I thought it was possible, I wouldn't do it. You haven't exactly made it easy for us to protect you. I simply can't trust you."

"And if you could? If I promised to follow the letter of the law? Would that buy me some time? You might have this all cleared up in a few days."

By sheer luck, maybe. Cam walked to the windows overlooking Central Park. The decision should have been simple. Protocol demanded that at the first sign of any threat she intensify the security measures around the subject. Not notifying her superiors would certainly place her own position in jeopardy. On the other hand, this was the first time she had even the slightest hint of cooperation from Blair Powell. She would need that cooperation if she was to have any chance at all of containing the situation. That made tactical sense, and, at least for the moment, she had plenty of manpower to stay within the margin of safety. From twenty stories up, she watched the horses and buggies winding their way through the lamp lit streets of the park. Across the room, Blair remained silent, but Cam could feel her gaze on her back. More than that, she could remember the look in her eyes. Blair had been vulnerable, and, more than that, afraid. Cam tried to pretend that didn't affect her decision.

"I'll keep it quiet for now, assuming there are no further threats." Cam turned from the window, her hands deep in her pockets. "As long as you cooperate with me."

"You've got a deal." Blair relaxed perceptibly.

"At the next sign of contact, I'll have to advise the chief of staff. That's the best I can do."

"Thank you."

Watching Blair intently, Cam leaned one shoulder against the wall. She'd been up all night the previous evening, chasing Blair and then chasing away Blair's ghost with sex. It was almost midnight.

She was bone tired, and she still had hours of work to do. "You have any idea who might be doing this?"

"Why should I?" Blair responded, surprised and defensive.

"This might not have been the first attempt at contact," Cam said gently. The quick flash of horror on Blair's face made her stomach clench. "Anyone strike you as behaving unusually?"

"No."

"Someone who tried to approach you—at the gym or the gallery, maybe in a bar?"

"No, no one."

"Someone you spent the night with?"

"You saw for yourself," Blair said steadily, her eyes fixed on Cam's face. "The women I go home with have no idea who I am. If they know anything at all, they know me by Allison."

"Your middle name," Cam observed. "And what about *their* names? Can you give me any kind of list, any addresses?"

"Not unless you think the names 'baby,' 'honey,' and 'sweetheart' will do you any good," Blair responded acerbically.

"What about someone you've seen more regularly?"

"There hasn't been anyone," Blair stated flatly.

Cam ran a hand through her hair and sighed involuntarily. She had hoped there might be a lead among Blair's sexual liaisons. If the stalker was indeed completely anonymous, unknown to Blair in any capacity, it would only be through serendipity that they would catch him—or her.

"All right then," Cam said. "When Mac gets back, I'll need you to look at the security tapes with us. Perhaps you'll recognize someone going in or out of the building."

"Fine." She felt like she'd been up for forty-eight hours, and looking at Cam, it was plain that she was exhausted, too. The agent's usually pristine suit was rumpled, and she had dark circles under her eyes. Blair had a sudden urge to brush the tousled hair back from her forehead. She had an even more disturbing desire to slip the suit jacket off Cam's shoulders and guide her toward the couch. The next moment, she saw herself unbuttoning Cam's shirt. She stood abruptly, forcing the images from her mind.

"I'm going to take a nap if you're going to have me up the rest of the night," she said curtly.

Cam glanced at Blair's stiff back as she crossed the room and slammed the bedroom door behind her. Then she slumped down on the couch tiredly, allowing herself a few minutes of rest before the long night began. The next thing she knew there was a knock at the door and movement in the room. She opened her eyes in time to see Blair about to open the door.

"Blair!" Cam was across the room before Blair could turn the knob. Grasping her forearm, Cam said sharply, "Let *me* do that."

"What?" Blair asked in surprise. The security chief had her gun drawn, and the look on her face was intent. For the first time, Blair truly appreciated the severity of the situation. She also understood that Cameron Roberts was completely serious about protecting her. The still-fresh scar on Cam's thigh was a lingering testimony to the woman's willingness to put herself in danger to protect another. Blair's stomach churned at the thought of Cam being wounded, and for a second, she hesitated, her hand still on the doorknob.

"Step behind me, please," Cam ordered steadily as she gently drew Blair's hand away. Putting herself between Blair and the door, her gun now at shoulder level, she said, "Who's there?"

"Stark and Mac," Mac replied.

Cam opened the door to the length of the security chain and peered out into the lighted hallway. Mac and the young female agent stood outlined in the doorway. She lowered her gun and opened the door to admit them. As they passed by, she briefly checked the hallway beyond, then reholstered her service automatic and secured the door.

"Have you got the tapes?"

"The tapes and dinner," Mac responded, unpacking several bags. He looked at his boss, knowing that she must be tired and hungry. The president's daughter was watching the commander, too. He couldn't quite describe the look on her face, but it seemed to be a mixture of fascination and uncertainty. There was something else there as well, something that reminded him of the way men looked at women. It was the first time he had ever seen anything so blatantly sexual between women. He wondered for a moment if the commander was aware of it, or even if Blair Powell was.

"Right," Cam said briskly. "Everybody grab whatever you want to eat and let's start looking at these tapes. Ms. Powell, I'm afraid I'm going to a have to ask you to sit through this with us. It will be tedious, but you may recognize someone."

"Of course," Blair said in a strangely subdued tone of voice. "Didn't someone promise me a Corona?'"

Cam looked at Mac with a raised eyebrow. "Mac?"

"Coming up," he said as he reached for the phone to call room service.

Three hours later, the pizza boxes were empty, a six-pack of Corona was gone, and daybreak was not far away. They had watched tapes from the previous two days and found nothing out of the ordinary. It was unlikely that anything would turn up in surveillance from earlier in the week, but they would review those tapes as well. Beginning with the morning shift, agents would begin the labor-intensive job of interviewing all of the building's employees as well as everyone known to have made deliveries.

"Let's take a break, everybody," Cam said with a sigh. "Mac, Stark, brief the others on what we need from the interviews. I'll stay here with Ms. Powell. Let's plan on another update at noon."

When the two agents left, Cam turned to Blair. "You should get some sleep. This afternoon, I want to go over anything you can remember from the past few weeks that might have been unusual."

"Right." Blair stopped at the door to the master suite, turning to look at Cam. Quietly, she said, "You should get some rest, too."

"My thoughts exactly." Cam smiled slightly and gave Blair an oddly gentle look. "I know this is hard for you. Just bear with me for a few days, and hopefully we can get back to normal."

"Normal?" Blair said with a tinge of sadness. "Commander, I wouldn't recognize it."

Cam stared thoughtfully after her as the door closed softly between them. She could feel Blair's loneliness linger in the air, and it felt surprisingly like her own. She pushed the thought away and stretched out on the couch, finally giving in to her fatigue.

When she awoke, momentarily disoriented, she found a light cover had been placed over her. The curtains were drawn, and the room was in near darkness. There was the sound of quiet breathing in the still room. After a moment, she could discern the shape of someone sitting nearby.

"Couldn't sleep?" Cam said into the darkness.

"No. I always have difficulty falling asleep anywhere other than my own bed." A hint of sarcastic laughter followed. "That's probably why I never spend the night with anyone."

"Leave the door open and try again," Cam suggested. "Sometimes just the sound of another's breathing is all we need to hear."

Blair was stunned. She hadn't meant to say anything, and the gentle response caught her off guard. She couldn't remember the last time she had allowed anyone this close. It frightened her, and she resorted automatically to her long-practiced defenses. "I think it might be better if you joined me in the bedroom. I can guarantee you at least one of us would sleep...eventually."

Cam shifted to a sitting position and spread her arms out along the back of the sofa. She could barely see Blair's face in the shadows. "I'm not available."

The words came quietly, and in a tone that might have suggested regret. Nevertheless, the rebuke stung. Blair knew that in her heart, her offer had been serious. She had wanted to fall asleep with Cam by her side.

"You certainly seemed available last night."

"That was just biology," Cam said calmly.

"Biology." Blair snorted. "Is that what we're calling it now? You were hot, and you were ready. Deny it if it makes you feel any better, but I *know* what I felt."

"I'm not denying anything. What I am saying is that nothing can happen between us."

"Relax, Commander. I'm not asking for a lifetime commitment." Blair eased herself out of the chair and approached the sofa. She leaned down, placing an arm on either side of Cam's body. Their faces were only inches apart. "Why pretend you don't want it?"

Cam remained motionless. The air around her was charged with sexuality. Heat radiated from Blair's body, and the faint scent of excitement caused her own blood to surge. She was quite sure, also, that Blair could tell she was aroused. She couldn't alter the pounding of her heart or the quickening of her breath. "What will it take to convince you?"

"Tell me you don't want me to touch you," Blair whispered as she leaned closer yet. "I can assure you, I am just as accomplished as any professional you might procure to take care of your needs."

"Ms. Powell, I do not want to have sex with you," Cam said in an even voice. She was surprised at the rapidity and accuracy of Blair's information gathering. She was far from embarrassed, however. There was very little difference between the casual sex that Blair enjoyed and what she herself sought in anonymity and privacy. "All I need from you is your cooperation."

Blair heard the finality in her voice. She had been rejected before, but never by anyone she wanted quite so much. What angered her the most was that she sensed Cam's desire. Cameron Roberts represented everything she could not have in her own life—independence, self-determination, and freedom. Knowing this fueled her urge to strip the self-contained agent of her restraint. For just those fleeting moments at the pinnacle of release, she'd wanted to hold Cam's will in her hands. At least that's how it had started.

Now, there was something else, something much more dangerous. Now she wanted the comfort of Cam's presence in the dark. Slowly, she straightened. "If you keep me cooped up in this place for very long, I won't be responsible for my actions."

"I promise to make this as short and painless as possible." Cam recognized the concession in her voice and laughed softly. "I'm sure you can be trusted, no matter how long it takes."

Don't be so sure, Commander. If I have to be this close to you twenty-four hours a day, I'm not sure I can trust myself.

CHAPTER EIGHT

Blair winced as Paula Stark led yet another ten in a suit where the aces hadn't yet been played. If she had to watch her "partner" make one more stupid play, she might have to take Mac's gun and shoot her.

Her patience was gone. She had not been out of the apartment in three days. They had just finished a dinner of Chinese takeout, and Cam had left Blair with Stark, Mac, and Taylor while she went to Blair's apartment building for a briefing with the other agents. Blair was keenly aware of her absence. The air seemed electric when Cam was around. She looked toward the door with relief when she heard the knock.

"How is your pinochle, Commander?" she asked as Cam crossed the room to join them.

Cam raised an inquiring eyebrow. "Are you playing for money?"

Blair laughed. "If we were, I'm afraid I'd be in big trouble."

"In that case, I'll play. Partners?"

Paula Stark pushed back from the table. "Please, take my place. I never was any good at cards, and I'm due back at the command center now anyways."

Cam sat down across from Blair. They played as if they had been playing together for years. Each time Cam bid, she had a sense that Blair knew exactly what she intended. It was both unsettling and exhilarating. Before long, Mac and Taylor were complaining that the two women had some kind of secret signal going. The score became so uneven that eventually they called it quits.

"I might have known you'd be a great partner, Commander," Blair said softly. "I'm sure you are equally good at everything."

Her tone was intimate and the suggestiveness did not escape Mac's notice. His boss seemed unaffected as she stood and stretched. She had shed her jacket, and the straps of her shoulder holster stretched her shirt tight over her torso. Mac didn't miss the way Blair's eyes flickered over Cam's body. *Christ, I'm surprised the commander doesn't go up in flames.*

If Cam had heard Blair's remark, or felt her appraising glance, she did not show it. She made no reply as she turned to her agents. "Why don't you two take a break for a few hours. Have one of the night crew come by around midnight. I'll be fine until then."

After the men left, Cam settled into a chair in the suite's large sitting area with the day's reports. Blair sat opposite her on the couch with a sketchpad. The room lights were low, and Cam's face was partially in shadow.

"Do you mind?" Blair asked as she began to draw.

Cam glanced over, smiled faintly, and went back to her reading. "No."

"Most people do," Blair said without looking up. She was sketching the fine straight nose, the deep-set dark eyes, and the chiseled cheekbones and jaw from memory. It was a face that had caught her attention the first time she'd seen it, and it never failed to entice her. It was a face meant to be drawn. Unfortunately, the more she saw her, the more exciting she found her. Cam was everything Blair found attractive in a woman, and the effect Cam had on her was unsettling. Their close proximity the last few days hadn't helped.

Blair found herself listening for Cam's voice when she awoke in the morning and looking for her whenever she entered a room. She found Cam's presence both disturbing and strangely reassuring, and she'd tried to discount her feelings by reminding herself that it was only natural to find a good-looking woman appealing. She simply chose to ignore her racing pulse and unmistakable arousal whenever Cam was near.

"I'm actually used to it," Cam remarked absently.

"Really?" Blair looked up at that.

"My mother is an artist."

Blair regarded her seriously. "Would I know her?"

"You might," Cam said softly, putting her papers aside. "Her name is Marcea Casells."

"You wouldn't be joking, would you?"

Cam shook her head.

"Well." Blair was momentarily at a loss. "I suppose I should be embarrassed to even let you see my work. She is quite... wonderful."

"Yes, she is." Cam thought of the canvases in Blair's loft. "From the little I have seen of your work, so are you. Of course, I'm no critic. I only know what I've seen of my mother's work, and that of her friends."

"Then you have been exposed to the best," Blair said lightly. "Did you grow up in Italy?"

"Yes, until I was twelve." A shadow flickered across Cam's face, then was gone. "After that, I was schooled in the United States."

Blair spoke aloud without thinking. "I remember hearing something about her husband—"

"My father was the American ambassador to Italy," Cam responded evenly. "He was killed in a terrorist car-bombing attack when I was eleven."

"Oh God, I'm sorry. I had forgotten." Blair regarded Cam with true anguish in her face. She'd been almost the same age when her own mother had died. After that, she'd been terrified that something would happen to her father. Growing up surrounded by armed guards hadn't made her feel any safer. Stubbornly, she never gave any thought to her own safety. To do so would have forced her to accept that the constraining security measures taken to protect her were actually necessary. "It must have been horrible for you."

"It was much harder for my mother." Cam looked into the distance, remembering. "They were completely devoted, and his death nearly destroyed her. If it hadn't been for her work, I don't think she would have survived."

"And she never remarried?" Blair questioned softly. She thought of her own father, alone for so many years. She had always thought it was his ambition that kept him from needing anyone, including her. Just another of the many reasons she resented being the president's daughter.

"No," Cam replied, her voice pensive. "I don't think anyone else would have compared."

"Are you like her?" Blair asked boldly. She couldn't help wondering about the death of the detective rumored to be Cam's lover. Perhaps the commander loved her still, and that was the reason she seemed immune to Blair's attentions. For an instant, Blair was jealous, and then berated herself for her foolishness.

"No, I'm not like her at all." Again, that fleeting smile. "My mother is an artist."

"Meaning?"

"She is a mysterious combination of deep passion, volatile sensitivities, and uncommon vision."

"Is that how you see artists?" Blair was fascinated, and suddenly, the answer mattered very much.

"Yes. I find them to be persons of rare fragility and unsurpassed emotional complexity." Cam focused on Blair's face, thinking not of her mother, but of Blair's indomitable spirit. "Hell to live with, but worth every moment of the knowing."

Blair felt Cam's words to her core. The intensity in her expression, the deep feeling in her voice, threatened to rock the foundation of Blair's world. She had never wanted anything more than she wanted Cameron Roberts to feel that way about her. It was impossible, and the last thing she wanted to feel. This need would make her weak. The longing would endanger what little independence she still had. Torn between the urge to flee and the physically painful attraction that was so much more than sexual, she wrenched her eyes away from Cam's compelling face.

"I can't draw you when you're talking," she said thickly as she focused on her charcoal and paper.

Cam watched Blair's delicate hand stroke the textured surface, thinking how beautiful and gifted she was. And what an emotional minefield. One moment she was heat and anger, the next an ember radiating sultry sensuality. Then just as suddenly, like now, withdrawn and somehow fragile. Her legs were curled under her, and she bent her upper body protectively over her work. Her blond hair fell free in riotous curls around her face, making her seem very young. She looked innocent, and terrifyingly vulnerable. Cam thought of the package left outside Blair's door, and her mind rebelled from the image of anyone harming her.

But then, she reminded herself, it was her responsibility to see that nothing and no one did. Cam returned to her reading absolutely certain that her sudden urge to run her hands through those curls was simply in response to their conversation and had nothing to do with the compelling beauty of the woman herself.

❖

At 7:00 the next morning, Cam walked out of the second bedroom after finishing a shower. Across the room, Blair and Paula Stark were so engrossed in conversation they didn't notice her. She couldn't hear them from where she was standing, but Blair had one hand on Stark's forearm and was peering intently into her face. It looked as if Stark was trying to back up, but Blair had effectively maneuvered her against the wet bar. Cam had witnessed this particular seduction before. She wasn't sure what made her angrier, Blair's obvious attention to the woman or the fact that her agent seemed to find the president's daughter fascinating. Any kind of romantic involvement between agents and the individuals they were guarding was strictly forbidden. It wasn't just policy, it made tactical sense. You couldn't be objective in a dangerous situation if you were personally, particularly intimately, involved with the subject.

Stark slipped past Blair to answer a knock at the door. Cam automatically stepped between Blair and the door, shielding her until she was certain it was Taylor. They had been there four days, and it was time for her to make a decision.

"We need to talk," she said to Blair.

Blair regarded her suspiciously, realizing Cam must have seen her with Stark. She hadn't really given much thought to the good-looking, dark-haired agent previously, although she had been aware of Stark shadowing her in the bars over the last few months. Stark was attractive, in a wholesome kind of way—well built, clear-eyed, and earnest. Blair had never really been interested in her sexually, probably because she guessed Stark wasn't a lesbian. She had learned at a very young age not to fool around with straight women. However, after having been cooped up in a three-room suite for four days with Cameron Roberts, a woman who seemed to turn her on without effort and rejected her with similar ease, Blair found herself trying to entice the younger agent out of boredom.

"It seems that one of the building cleaning employees delivered the package to your door," Cam reported. "An unidentified boy apparently gave her ten dollars to do it. In all probability, the stalker used the boy as a go-between so he couldn't be described. We don't have either of them on video, and there's no way we're going to ID the boy."

"So it's a dead end?"

"Unfortunately, yes."

"Then I can go home?" Blair asked, finding that she had mixed feelings about that. She was sick to death of being confined with people constantly around her, and she missed the freedom to work. On the other hand, Cam had rarely left the hotel in the four days they had been there. When Cam needed to sleep, she had several of the other agents stand guard. Blair had gotten used to her presence. The security chief was there when Blair woke up, and when she went to bed. In the many hours in between, they had talked together, read together, and shared silences together. It was the most intimate time she had spent with anyone since her days in school.

"I'd rather you didn't go back to the apartment immediately," Cam replied. "I think it would be best if you took some time away. That would give us a chance to finish our interviews with neighbors and delivery people we missed in the first sweep. A trip out of town might be good idea."

"Diane and I had discussed going skiing," Blair mused. "Now might be the perfect time. I'll call her and arrange something for next weekend."

Cam nodded in agreement. "That would work. The weekend might be a little too soon, since I'll need advance notice to inform the resort and work out the shift details."

"You can do that on the plane," Blair said with a hint of irritation. She wasn't used to altering her plans or delaying to accommodate her security teams.

"May I remind you that we have an agreement," Cam commented quietly.

"I think I agreed not to give your agents the slip," Blair responded pointedly.

"Actually, I believe you agreed to give us your cooperation," Cam countered, "*as well* as not giving us the slip."

"Next time it will have to be in writing," Blair muttered. Catching the quick smile that flashed across Cam's handsome features, she laughed in spite of herself. "How about if we work out the details tonight—over dinner?"

"All right." Cam knew she had been outmaneuvered, but accepted the token of cooperation. She started to turn away, then added, "This is the first field assignment of this caliber for several of my people. It wouldn't look good for them if I had to reassign them."

"And why might you need to do that?" Blair asked suspiciously.

"If one of them were to compromise their objectivity, say, through a *friendship* with you—just for an example."

"Friendship? Or sex?"

"Either."

"Aren't you worried about yourself, then?" Blair asked angrily, resenting the implied restriction. She might have promised cooperation, but she didn't pledge celibacy. "As I recall, we've already been *friendly.*"

"I'm not a rookie, Ms. Powell," Cam answered smoothly as she turned away. "I can resist temptation."

Blair stared after her, seething. If she wanted to bed Paula Stark in the middle of the hotel lobby, she damn well would. Cameron Roberts might have control over her time, but she would never have control over anything that really mattered to her.

❖

Blair spent the rest of the day getting settled back into her apartment, and she didn't see Cam again. She hadn't forgotten, however, that they had dinner plans. She dressed carefully, ignoring the quick thud of her pulse when her doorbell rang at 6:30 p.m.

"Let's walk," Blair said by way of greeting. As usual, her security chief looked enormously attractive in a khaki blazer, plain blue shirt, and pressed stone-washed jeans. Blair tried not to pay any attention to the faint hint of cologne that registered pleasantly in the air…and other places.

"All right."

Blair draped her wool overcoat on her arm and eyed Cam speculatively. "Need a jacket?"

"I'll be fine," Cam replied. "Warm-blooded."

"I'll bet."

Cam laughed, noting, as they crossed to the elevator, the way Blair's silk jacket and trousers enhanced her lithe form. Her hair was down, too, giving her that slightly abandoned look that was so damn sexy. *Remember what you warned her about friendships. Jesus.*

Blair moved gracefully, with easy confidence, and Cam knew it was because she was going out not as Blair Powell, the president's daughter, but as an ordinary twenty-five-year-old woman going to dinner. For an instant, Cam regretted her job. She wished she could view the evening ahead as simply a date with a beautiful woman. But she couldn't. Even though Blair could forget, or try to forget, who she was—ignoring the very real threats that existed in her life by pursuing a never-ending series of sexual conquests to prove her independence—Cam couldn't forget. No matter what face Blair chose to show the outside world, Cam knew her to be the many-faceted, talented, and complicated woman she was sworn to protect. And that's *all* she could be.

Nevertheless, when Blair turned to her in the elevator and favored her with a smile, Cam smiled back. And despite her reservations and responsibilities, she found herself looking forward to dinner with a sense of anticipation that she hadn't known in years.

As the elevator came to a halt and the doors began to slide open, Blair placed her hand on Cam's forearm. With an undertone of urgency in her voice, she said, "I don't want the rest of the team to come with us."

"Ms. Powell, I—"

"Please. I've been watched constantly for days with near-strangers supervising every moment." Blair's eyes met Cam's. "I just want a few hours alone to have dinner with you."

"I know how hard it's been," Cam responded quietly. "But I can't let you go unprotected. Not now, especially so soon after that package was delivered. I'll tell them to stay out of sight."

"It's not the same."

"I know it isn't. Believe me, Blair, if I could change it, I would."

Perhaps it was the way Cam said her name, her *first* name. None of the Secret Service ever used it. Perhaps it was the sincerity in her voice. It was enough. Blair brushed her fingers along Cam's sleeve, touching the back of Cam's hand with her fingertips for just a moment. "Thank you."

Cam whispered a few words into her microphone as she stepped out of the elevator to take Blair's arm. She wasn't entirely certain this was a good idea, but she had a feeling if she didn't allow Blair this small bit of independence, she would lose whatever chance she had of Blair's cooperation. In truth, she didn't have the heart to keep her constrained any longer. It wasn't just the last four days, it was the last thirteen years.

As they walked out into the chill early-evening air, Cam realized how much she wanted to give Blair these few moments of happiness. She caught her breath in surprise when Blair slipped her fingers into her hand, all too aware that at least three of her agents were watching.

"You like to live dangerously, Ms. Powell."

"I didn't think you were afraid of rumors, Commander," Blair said tauntingly.

"It's not the rumors I'm afraid of," Cam said dryly. "It's your father."

The agents threading their way through the crowd ten feet behind looked at each other curiously, wondering what had prompted the unrestrained laughter from Blair Powell.

❖

"All right. I think we can manage it," Cam said as she leaned back in her chair. She sipped her espresso, comfortably relaxed after a slow, quiet dinner in a small restaurant off Fourth Street in the West Village. They shared a table for two in front of a large, open wood-burning fireplace. Blair had initially requested a table in the wide front window, but Cam had politely declined, requesting seating where Blair wasn't quite so exposed.

"I'm glad you agree," Blair said with a hint of laughter. For once, it didn't bother her that she had to clear her plans with her security chief. Even *she* had to admit that Cam wasn't being unreasonable.

"It will still take a day or two to get everything into place," Cam warned.

"I'll practice patience." Blair sipped her cognac and studied her dinner companion. For two hours they had talked of art, which cities they enjoyed most in Europe, and the comparative value of various martial art forms. What they had not discussed was politics, the stalker situation, or their personal lives. It could easily have passed for a first date, filled with the anticipation and excitement of learning to know someone new. She felt like someone she barely recognized and didn't want reality to dispel the myth too soon. "I appreciate you rushing the plans."

"Since you've been so *cooperative,* it's the least I can do," Cam teased lightly.

The grin that tugged at the corner of Cameron Roberts's mouth was enough to make Blair's blood race. She smiled back, wondering at the quick surge of pleasure that wasn't sexual, but still enormously satisfying. Then, with a jolt, it occurred to her that what was missing was the burning anger, her constant companion. That in and of itself was frightening. If she allowed herself to get used to this feeling, the emptiness and disappointment of her real life would be devastating. She was acutely aware of Cam's gaze drifting over her face. Cam had a way of looking at her that made her feel like there was no one else in the room; her glance as palpable as a caress. For an instant, Blair imagined that her skin tingled where Cam's eyes lingered. She struggled to keep her tone normal.

"I spoke with Diane this afternoon. She can't wait to go."

"I'll get the team working on the arrangements first thing in the morning," Cam assured her.

"She told me she saw you today," Blair added nonchalantly. That was far from the way she had felt when Diane casually remarked that she had had lunch with Cameron Roberts.

"Yes. We had a bit of business to do."

"I'm sure," Blair said sarcastically. She knew very well the kind of business Diane had in mind. She also knew exactly the kind of woman Diane found attractive. Over the years, they had often found themselves in competition for the same women. When they were younger it had all been in fun, with no hard feelings whatever happened. This time, it felt like anything but fun. Angry at herself for allowing her irritation to show, Blair kept her eyes fixed on the dark swirling liquid in her glass, afraid of what her companion might see in her face.

Cam had a pretty good idea what Diane had insinuated about their lunch. The charming art dealer had certainly made her interests quite obvious. Cam hadn't been offended by the blatant attempt at seduction, but she did not want Blair, for reasons she could not clearly define, to think she was so easily seduced.

"You know, Ms. Powell," Cam said gently, "sometimes a cigar *is* just a cigar."

"I can't believe you just said that!" Blair laughed, coaxed out of her anger by the ridiculousness of the image.

"Neither can I." Cam laughed with her, thinking how luminescent Blair's features were when she relaxed. "But in this case, it's apt."

"I promise not to tell her," Blair confided, still smiling. "A woman scorned, and all."

Grinning, Cam inclined her head gratefully. "Thank you."

With a sense of regret, Cam accepted the check from the waiter. Glancing at Blair in the glow of the candlelight, she felt an unfamiliar ache. When Blair's eyes met hers, Cam suddenly recognized the feeling—she saw it reflected in the beautiful face. Loneliness, and desire. "Are you ready to go?"

"No," Blair said softly. "No, not at all."

They were both silent as Cam helped Blair into her coat and they walked out into one of those rare January nights when the stars could actually be seen over New York City. Blair actually forgot for a moment that there were three Secret Service agents dogging their every step. The meal had been wonderful, and the company even better. She stopped in mid-step. Taking a chance, she asked, "I don't suppose I could interest you in a trip to the bar?"

Cam took a deep breath of the brisk air, searching for a way to answer that would not destroy their fragile truce. What Blair was asking for was more than a nightcap. Alone, in a bar, there was too much chance for casual intimacy, too much chance for a brief caress. For a second she remembered the way Blair's hands had felt on her the last time they met in the shadows. She shook her head, ignoring the quick surge of desire, refusing to acknowledge her own wishes. "I can't accompany you. But if you want to go out, I will see that the team is as discreet as possible."

"You didn't mind having dinner with me," Blair pointed out, still not moving, not caring that they were creating a minor obstacle to other passersby. She didn't want their evening to end. Her quiet dinner with Cam had been far more exciting than some breathless coupling with a nameless stranger.

"That was business," Cam responded. *Christ, now you're lying to her. And at least she asked to go out. Every other time, she's just slipped away.*

"Was it?"

"No." Cam knew very well she had stretched the definition of "business." They could have discussed the upcoming ski trip in the morning, but she had allowed the excuse of the trip to give her a reason to have dinner with Blair. She was on dangerous ground, and she could not let things progress further. She certainly could not go to a gay bar with Blair as anything resembling her date. *And God knows I can't go cruising with her. Watching her pick up strangers for sex is going to drive me crazy.*

"Then say yes, Cam. Come with me."

"I *can't,*" Cam said intently. "I'm sorry."

"Are you?" Blair asked softly, searching Cam's face.

Cam avoided her eyes. She'd said too much already. A muscle in her jaw jumped as she asked, "Do you want me to notify the unit that you'll be staying out?"

"No, thanks," Blair said bitingly. "When I go out, I don't want the company of the Secret Service."

Cam supposed she deserved that. "Then may I walk you home?"

"Yes," Blair said with a sigh. "But for God's sake, tell them to stay off our heels. I'm perfectly safe with you."

Cam nodded, whispering instructions into her microphone. She appreciated that Blair could have been difficult about this. She was grateful that she would not have to worry about Blair's whereabouts, at least for the rest of evening. And even more, she was thankful she would not have to worry about with whom Blair would spend the night.

Chapter Nine

Several days later, they boarded a chartered jet for their flight to Colorado. Their destination was a small, rustic resort not usually known as a tourist center. It was Blair's choice, and fortunately, likely to be less crowded and an easier setting in which to provide security. It was a fairly isolated location, far from any large cities, with few of the amenities so popular in Colorado ski resorts. There would be no nightly entertainment acts or other similar diversions. What there *would* be was hours of good skiing on challenging trails. For Blair and Diane Bleeker, it might be a vacation, but for Cam and her agents, it would be anything but. Arrangements had to be made for emergency transport from the hard-to-reach locale, the local police had to be notified of possible road closures in the event of evacuation, and surveillance points had to be mapped out in unfamiliar terrain. The team had worked long hours on short notice seeing to the details.

Cam settled into her seat and was just opening the *Washington Chronicle* when someone eased in beside her.

"This seat looks vacant," a familiar voice announced.

"These are not reserved seats." Cam shifted to smile at Diane Bleeker. "Good morning."

"Then I take it you don't mind the company?" Diane smiled and brushed her hair back with a perfectly manicured hand.

"Not at all," Cam responded, folding her paper. "Whatever news there might be, it can wait until later."

Diane went in search of her seat-belt, brushing her hand along the length of Cam's thigh as she did. She noted a subtle tensing under her fingertips, but Cameron Roberts, to her credit, did not pull away. Diane could accept rejection, but she hated to have her advances ignored. She allowed her hand to linger a moment longer, then slowly removed it and extracted the seat-belt from between them. "Do you ski, Commander?"

"Yes, I do."

"Our Blair is quite the expert, did you know?"

"It doesn't surprise me," Cam commented. "She's very talented."

"She likes to ski the unmarked trails. She's very adventurous that way."

"I don't doubt it."

Diane studied the dark gray eyes, searching for hidden meaning. She couldn't remember ever having met anyone quite so inscrutable. And yet the agent was anything but cold. She radiated vigor, displayed daunting self-confidence, and seemed to do everything with an intense focus. Even though Cameron Roberts *was* enormously attractive with her lean, tautly muscled body and roguish good looks, it was more than simple physical appeal. The woman *seethed* with promise, the promise of passion, and that was something Diane very much wanted to experience. And as she was coming to expect, she could read nothing in Cam's expression. *Is there nothing that can shake her composure?*

"Yes, Blair is a woman of many hidden skills." Diane leaned against Cam's shoulder as she tightened her seat-belt. "Then again, she doesn't bother to hide some of her interests. I'm sure you've noticed."

Cam had no intention of discussing Blair Powell with Diane Bleeker or anyone else. "And how is the gallery? Business good, I hope?"

"Ah, I see," Diane murmured, casually pressing her breast against Cam's arm. "Our Blair is off limits. Actually, that's perfectly all right with me. I'm much more interested in you."

Cam laughed at the woman's persistence. It was hard to be annoyed with someone who was so blatant about her intentions. In another place, in another time, she would not have resisted. It was a combination of the past, and her strange detached present, which prevented her from responding. Any kind of intimate involvement, any meaningful connection at all, was beyond her capability. In the months since Janet's death, she couldn't bring herself to touch a woman in any but the most superficial way. Her impersonal arrangement with Claire satisfied her physical needs, and she contented herself with that. She was functioning, she could work, and that was all she wanted. Quickly dispelling the memories, Cam warned, "I'm afraid I'm going to disappoint you."

"Oh, I very seriously doubt that."

"I'm flattered—" Cam began.

Diane laughed. "Oh please, Commander. You needn't explain to me the many reasons why you *think* you are unavailable. I am quite patient, and I enjoy the chase. Otherwise, where is the pleasure when you win?"

Cam shook her head, smiling at the sophisticated, supremely confident woman beside her. "Then I shall say no more."

"Good." Diane wrapped her long, elegant fingers around Cam's wrist, squeezing gently before slowly withdrawing. "It would be to no avail."

They both settled back in their seats for takeoff. In the aisle seat one row behind them, Blair studied the two women. She was completely familiar with Diane's tactics. She had known her since they were girls and had witnessed her many conquests. This was the first time it mattered to her whether Diane succeeded. The image of Diane's hand on Cam's arm provoked a response she was finding hard to ignore. She hated the thought of Diane touching Cam, but she found it even harder to accept the possibility of Cam returning the caresses. Instinctively, she knew that Cameron Roberts would not make love to a woman casually. What she couldn't know was how much that fact controlled Cam's life.

❖

The group was greeted at the door to the lodge by a brunette in her mid-forties, who, even in winter, showed signs of a lingering tan. Her lithe, trim figure bespoke her vigorous lifestyle. She greeted them warmly and ushered them into a rustic room scattered with sofas and comfortable-looking overstuffed chairs arranged in front of a large stone fireplace. It was late afternoon, and a fire blazed on the hearth. Overhead lights, hidden in the exposed wooden beams of the ceiling, were turned on low and, in conjunction with the last rays of sunlight slanting through huge windows, bathed the room in a muted golden glow.

"I'm Doris Craig," she said, extending her hand as Cam stepped over the threshold. "Just leave your gear here until we have the room situation straightened out. Then I'll have someone bring your bags up."

She looked from Cam to Blair, who was standing just to Cam's right. Of course, Doris recognized her and had expected Blair's entourage. Without a trace of shyness, Doris offered her hand again. "I'm delighted to have you here, Ms. Powell. We have eighteen inches of packed snow with a three-inch fresh fall from last night. The trails are perfect."

"Just the news I wanted to hear." Blair grinned, pleased at Doris's lack of pretension and the genuine warmth in her greeting. "I can't wait to get out there."

Doris nodded in perfect understanding. "First light at 5:30 tomorrow. After you're settled and have some dinner, I'll show you the trail maps. You can plan your course for the morning."

"I was hoping to get in a run or two this afternoon."

"Well, it'll be dark in an hour and a half. If you hurry, you could ski one of the shorter trails."

"Just give me someplace to change," Blair said as she reached for her gear bag.

Doris noticed the sudden tension in the group of individuals standing around Blair, but it seemed to her that this was Blair Powell's party, and if she wanted to ski, she should certainly be able to ski. "Right this way."

As Blair followed Doris across the room and disappeared down a hallway, Cam turned to the others. She worked to keep her temper in check and her worry under wraps. *We've been here all of ten minutes, and she's already heading off on an unsecured jaunt. Jesus H. Christ.*

"All right, everybody—let's move. Mac, you take care of the room arrangements—preferably everyone on one floor. Make sure we have someone on either side of Egret's room, and across the hall." Searching for her own gear amidst the pile on the floor, she added, "Stark, Taylor, you get suited up and find out which trail she's going to run, then follow us out. Make sure you take an emergency kit with you. I'm going to change now so I can ski with her."

As usual, Blair's lack of regard for the realities of providing her protection had placed them in a difficult situation. They had no time to adequately survey the area, and they had no sense of who might be out on the trails with her. Cam was startled to feel the touch on her arm and stopped walking abruptly. For a moment, she had forgotten completely about Diane Bleeker.

"I should think you would be used to her by now, Commander," Diane said softly. "As long as I've known her, she has refused to accept that she cannot behave like the rest of the world. She has always wanted to be simply ordinary."

"She'll never be ordinary," Cam said softly. She thought of her own childhood and of what it had been like growing up among her father's diplomatic friends and her mother's world-famous artists' circle. She remembered watching the other children walk to school from the windows of the limousine that took her almost everywhere. She had longed to be one of the anonymous crowd, knowing all the time that it was impossible. She knew the sadness of being different, and the loneliness of being separate, no matter how hard her parents tried to create the appearance of an ordinary life. And she had been only a diplomat's daughter. *God, what must it have been like for Blair?*

Diane watched the emotions flickering quickly through Cam's dark eyes, astounded at the depth of the other woman's compassion and understanding, and a little frightened by her own response. She had long since abandoned the desire for anything beyond a casual physical relationship with the women in her life, but this one was different. There was something almost hypnotic in Cam's reserve, something tantalizing in her secrecy. She made you want to know her, without consciously inviting you near.

"If you'll excuse me," Cam said politely as she turned away, her mind on Blair.

"Of course. I'm sure Blair needs you." Diane was surprised to realize that she meant it, and as she watched the dark-haired agent stride away, for one of the few times in her life, she envied her old friend.

❖

"God, that was great!" Blair exclaimed, stomping the snow from her boots and shedding her ski parka. She made her way to the small bar tucked into one corner of the huge lobby. "I'd love a glass of red wine," she said to the bartender. She turned to Diane and Cam. "What about you two?"

"Martini for me," Diane said.

"Just coffee," Cam responded.

"That's a fabulous trail, don't you think?" Blair enthused, tossing her head back and shaking her hair free. Her eyes were glowing, her cheeks faintly flushed from the cold air.

"It was everything it was advertised to be," Cam responded. She had been skiing since she was three, and it had taken every bit of her skill to keep up with Blair. The younger woman was not only expert, but not surprisingly, she was fearless. Even in the waning light of late afternoon, she had blasted down the unfamiliar trail with abandon.

Diane, also a very accomplished skier, had followed several hundred yards behind them, skiing efficiently but much more cautiously. Cam had posted agents at the head and foot of the trail, in constant communication with her via radio, but she was the only one actually in near physical contact with Blair. Despite the low risk factor of this secluded resort, she did not want Blair very far from her sight. She hadn't skied quite so aggressively in ten years. She knew her muscles would be sore in the morning. Nevertheless, the sight of Blair's pleasure made it worth it. She was absolutely radiant, and Cam had a glimpse of what she might be like were the circumstances different. There was a joy and lightness about her that Cam had not seen before. Blair was more than beautiful; she was breathtaking.

Cam forced her gaze away from the president's daughter and gently placed her coffee cup on the bar top. "I think I'm ready for a shower."

"Will you be down for dinner, Commander?" Blair asked quietly. She had loved the skiing, but she'd loved the company more. Every time she'd looked over and seen Cam's tight form tracking by her side, she'd felt more complete than she'd ever imagined.

"Yes," Cam replied before she turned slightly and murmured into her lapel microphone. Almost instantly, a stocky red-haired man appeared in the doorway. Satisfied that her replacement was nearby, she walked away.

Blair watched her leave. Diane did, too, wondering if the Secret Service agent had any idea just how revealing the expression in her dark eyes could be. When Cam looked at Blair, the pleasure in her gaze was painfully evident. As quickly as it appeared, however, it was gone. Diane wondered what force of will it took for Cam to control her feelings so completely. She wondered too, why it was necessary.

CHAPTER TEN

Shortly after 5:00 the next morning, Blair pushed open the swinging doors to the kitchen and followed the scent of coffee. She found Doris seated at a scarred wooden table that would easily seat sixteen, sipping the steaming brew and working on a crossword puzzle. Doris smiled a greeting and gestured toward the coffeepot.

"Thanks," Blair grunted, reaching for a cup. Moving slowly, she sank down beside Doris at the table.

"Morning." When she got no reply, she waited until the Blair had taken a sip of coffee, then asked, "Where are your friends?"

Blair grimaced, blowing across the top of the liquid to cool it. "I'm sure there's someone right outside the back door and another one in the dining room."

"Doesn't seem like much fun."

"Not exactly." Blair appraised her cautiously. She saw no hint of anything other than friendliness in her expression and frankness in her tone. She allowed herself a brief smile. "Well, I could lie and say I'm used to it. In fact, I *am* used to it, but I've never learned to ignore it. It bothers me."

"I can imagine. On the other hand, I guess it *is* impossible to let you run around by yourself."

"Apparently so." Blair laughed, one of the rare times she considered her own circumstances without an accompanying rush of resentment. "My security chief would certainly agree."

"Agent Roberts?"

"Yes."

"I *did* notice she seems rather intent on your well-being." There was no hint of innuendo in her voice.

To her utter consternation, Blair blushed.

"That must be comforting," Doris added, "when it isn't annoying you."

"Yes," Blair whispered, wondering if the woman was a mind reader.

Doris leaned back, scrutinizing the striking young woman across from her. This was not the sophisticated, perfectly turned out celebrity she was used to seeing on the television and in magazine articles. This woman was naturally beautiful, with no make-up, untamed hair, faded jeans and a baggy sweatshirt that did little to hide the suggestive swell of her breasts. Doris would never have recognized her as the president's daughter. But she would not have overlooked her allure either.

"May I ask how you came to stay here?" Doris asked.

"A friend of mine, Tanner Whitley, has stayed here."

Doris raised an eyebrow slightly, remembering the attractive young business magnate from earlier in the season. "One of my most exciting guests," she responded. "She was here with another very striking woman, as I recall."

"Tanner usually is." Blair met her gaze evenly and was pleased to see that the other woman did not avert her eyes.

"You needn't be concerned about my discretion, Ms. Powell. My only interest is in providing my guests with good skiing and privacy. My only *hope* is that you have seven days of excellent running. I couldn't care less about your personal life."

Blair laughed. "Well, you may be the only person in the United States for whom that's true."

"I think you may be right." Doris laughed with her.

❖

An hour later, Cam walked into the lounge and helped herself to a cup of coffee from the large urn that stood always ready on the sideboard. She turned, sipping gratefully at the aromatic brew, and met the eyes of Doris Craig, who was working at a small desk tucked into one corner of the room. Doris smiled pleasantly, and Cam nodded as she settled into one of the large leather chairs before the fireplace. After a moment, Doris joined her with her own coffee.

"She's already out on the slopes," Doris commented. It hadn't taken her long the evening before to determine just who was giving the orders among the group of people surrounding Blair Powell.

"Yes, I know."

"I suppose you do," Doris said softly. "It must be very difficult for her."

Cam had been doing her job too many years to fall into the trap of casual conversation with a stranger. Especially a conversation about someone as high profile as the president's daughter. However, there was something so genuine about the woman beside her, she felt strangely at ease. "I imagine it is."

Doris might not have had any experience with the complicated relationships between a woman like Blair and those who guarded her, but she had plenty of experience with the attractions of one woman for another. She had had the opportunity to observe the reserved Secret Service agent and the first daughter together the previous night at dinner, and later in the evening when the group had gathered in the lounge. Blair Powell had scarcely taken her eyes off the charismatic security chief, and it seemed that Blair's best friend Diane was captivated as well. The object of their attention, however, had revealed little, unless you were watching her. And Doris had been watching her closely.

When the others were engaged in conversation, the dark-haired woman with the smoky gray eyes watched the president's daughter with a penetrating intensity that should have left marks on her skin. Doris had seen that look before, in the eyes of women who thought they knew their own hearts, and their own minds. In the eyes of women who refused to acknowledge the truth of their own feelings.

"It must be lonely for her," Doris remarked quietly. "She could probably use a friend."

"She has friends." Cam sighed and gently replaced her cup on the coffee table. She walked toward the fireplace, watching the bark glow red and crumble from the logs as they burned brightly to their own destruction. "What she needs is to be free. That's something no one can give her."

"There are more ways than one to be free."

Cam watched the fire burn for a long time, knowing she had no answers. When she turned around, she found she was alone.

❖

"It's beautiful, isn't it?" Blair commented as she joined Cam on the wide front deck of the ski lodge after dinner that night. The temperature was frigid, the air so crisp it tingled against her skin. The sky was impossibly black with stars so bright and so numerous it felt as if she were standing on the edge of heaven.

"Yes," Cam said pensively. "It is."

"You really shouldn't let Stark play pinochle." Their breath left small clouds of white crystals hanging in the air. Despite the temperature, she was not cold. She had been waiting all evening for an opportunity to be alone with her security chief. Now that the time had come, her pulse raised and her stomach stirred with an excitement she couldn't ignore. "She's god-awful and a danger to herself. If she had been my partner, I would have murdered her."

"Card playing is a necessity for a Secret Service agent," Cam responded seriously, although the corners of her mouth turned up in a smile.

"Yes, I'm sure." Blair stepped closer until her shoulder brushed Cam's, surprised when Cam did not move away. "Then again, I'm sure that Secret Service agents need to be talented in many things."

"Merely diligent." Cam sighed. "Don't stay outside too long, Ms. Powell. It's colder than it seems."

"There are remedies for that, you know." She rested her ungloved hand on Cam's bare wrist.

"Blair, I know how difficult all of this is for you—"

"I don't think you do," Blair said, stepping closer until they were face to face, their thighs lightly touching. "It's damned inconvenient finding a way to get one's security chief into bed without creating a national scandal."

"Perhaps there's a message there." Cam backed away just enough to break their contact. It was too hard for her to think with the heat of Blair's skin on hers.

"There may be, but I have no interest in it. All I'm interested in is you." Blair leaned forward, her lips very close to Cam's as she whispered, "Come to my room tonight, Cam. Please."

"I'm afraid you have mistaken my attentions," Cam said quietly. Blair Powell was easily the most attractive woman she had ever known, and if that wasn't enough, she was touchingly vulnerable in her unguarded moments. Cam wished there were some way to ease the younger woman's pain, but she could not allow her sympathy to interfere with her effectiveness. She reminded herself that the beautiful seductress was less interested in her than in using her as the tool to break the chains of her invisible prison. She didn't even blame her, but reminding herself of it helped her to ignore the hammering of her heart and the rush of blood into her depths. "Your physical well-being is my only concern. I am *not* interested in anything other than that."

The words ripped through Blair, causing her to flinch. She had not approached a woman with true desire in more years then she could count. It hurt, this rebuke. The pain, and the fact that she'd left herself open to it, angered her. As she turned and walked rapidly toward the door, she called caustically, "Don't mistake lust for affection, Commander. My interest in you, as I believe you once said, is strictly biological."

Cam watched her go, struggling with her own disappointment and, undeniably, her regret. Of course she knew that she was only a potential conquest, but that did not lessen the sting of Blair's words.

❖

A knock on Cam's door brought her from deep sleep into adrenalized alertness in an instant. She grabbed her gun from the night table as her feet touched the floor. The bedside clock read 4:44 a.m. She looked through the peephole, relieved to see that the figure on the other side was not the shift leader of Blair's detail. *Blair is all right.*

Cam opened the door an inch and whispered, "What is it, Stark?"

Paula Stark stared white-faced at her chief. She swallowed once audibly, and licked her suddenly dry lips nervously. "I need to talk you, Commander."

"Can't it wait?"

"No, ma'am, it can't."

"All right, Agent, come in." Cam opened the door to admit her subordinate, then replaced her gun in its holster on her bedside table. She switched on the lamp and motioned Stark to a chair at the small desk in front of the windows. She sat down across from Stark and looked at her inquiringly. For a moment, she thought that Stark might cry.

"I need to be transferred," Stark stated flatly.

"Is there some reason you felt you needed to wake me in the middle of the night to tell me this?" Cam asked sharply. She had a bad feeling she knew where this conversation was going.

"I needed to tell you now. I need to leave first thing in the morning."

Cam sighed and leaned back from the table. She ran both hands briskly over her face, then peered intently at the pale young woman across from her. "Do you want to tell me what this is all about?"

"I—I don't feel I can continue to carry out my assignment."

"That's not what you told me the day I arrived."

Paula Stark raised her eyes to Cam's for the first time. Her shoulders stiffened slightly. "I hadn't slept with her then."

Something hard settled deep in the pit of Cam's stomach. She clenched her jaw to stifle the curse that leapt to her lips. She stood abruptly, knocking her chair back a foot, and paced to the other side of the room. Then she turned so quickly in the small space that Stark flinched. "Are you out of your goddamned mind?"

"Commander...I...I have no excuse, ma'am." Stark stood on shaky legs. "I'll send my resignation as soon—"

"*Sit down.*" Cam fisted her hands, seething with fury, her formidable composure strained to the breaking point. She knew instinctively she was handling this poorly, but her immediate reaction was one of deep-seated anger, and, uncomfortably, something that felt a great deal like jealousy. "How in the *hell* did this happen?"

"It wasn't planned. It—I don't know—it just, she—" Stark raised her hands in a helpless gesture. "I walked her to her room, and then we were talking, and then she kis—"

"I don't want those details," Cam snapped.

Once again, Stark stiffened, but her eyes were clear and her voice steady when she answered, "She asked me, and I didn't say no."

"Jesus Christ," Cam muttered. *Is there no end to the chaos that woman can create? Now I've got to deal with the potential ruin of a very capable young woman's career.* "Who else knows?"

"No one. I waited until the hall was clear to leave her room."

Cam forced herself to think beyond her rage. Stark's future depended upon it. "How do you feel about her now?"

Stark looked at her chief in surprise. It was as if she had never considered the question before. "I don't know."

"Are you in love with her?" Cam asked quietly. For some reason, the words were hard to get out.

"I don't think so," Stark said, clearly embarrassed. "It was—physical."

"Yes, I'm sure it was," Cameron said under her breath. She refused to think about the two of them together, but it was difficult keeping the image of Blair making love with this woman from her mind. She shook her head, forcing herself to deal with the real issues at hand. "I wish that there was some way I could overlook this, Agent Stark, but I can't. Even if you have no personal feelings for her, I can't trust you to be objective. I can't trust you not to allow your relationship with her to cloud your judgment. It could be dangerous for her—and it could be dangerous for you."

"I know that, Commander." Stark looked down at her folded hands resting on the tabletop, her expression one of abject misery. "I've thought of nothing else for the last three hours. Ever since we...ever since...I've been agonizing over what to do."

"Why did you tell me?"

"Because if you found out and I *hadn't* told you, it would ruin my credibility forever," Stark replied instantly, her tone surprised. "I made a mistake, but I know my duty."

"Do you?" Cam regarded her with growing respect. To Stark's credit, she did not drop her gaze as Cam studied her unwaveringly in the lengthening silence. "Can you swear to me that there is no romantic attachment between you and Ms. Powell?"

"Yes, ma'am, I swear."

"You may continue with your post, Agent Stark. If I find that your judgment or performance is compromised in any way, I will transfer you immediately without regard for its impact on your career."

"Yes, ma'am. I understand, ma'am." Stark stood, nearly at attention. "Thank you so much."

Cam nodded, suddenly weary. As the door closed behind the young agent, Cam stretched out on the bed and stared at the ceiling. She ached inside, an ache of loss for something she hadn't even known she'd needed. Eventually she closed her eyes and tried to ignore the image of Blair Powell naked, her legs entwined with the shadowy figure of Paula Stark. Sleep wouldn't come, and eventually she rose, showered, and went downstairs to greet the dawn.

❖

"May I join you?"

"If you wish."

Blair did not miss the stiffness in Cam's voice, nor the cold, smoldering anger in her eyes. "I take it you know I had company last night."

"I am aware of it."

For some reason, Blair took no satisfaction in making it clear to her aloof security chief that Cam was not irreplaceable, especially in her bed. In fact, she had been plagued by an unfamiliar uneasiness throughout a restless night. For the first time in her memory, she felt regret about one of her sexual dalliances. Regret that the entire time she had made love to Paula Stark, she had wished for another's body beneath her lips, beneath her fingers. Regret that even as the young woman lay spent and vulnerable in her arms, she felt no love for her. Regret that the woman she had taken to her bed had been cheated by that very fact.

"You realize that you put her career in jeopardy?" Cam gritted her teeth, trying desperately to control her temper. She wasn't certain with whom she was most angry—Paula Stark for her lack of judgment or Blair Powell for her total lack of discretion in choosing her bed partners. Looking at Blair, Cam had to struggle even now not to imagine those soft sensuous lips on her body. She had known Blair's embrace, however fleetingly, and, despite her anger, she found it difficult to banish the memory. "Stark…Jesus Christ."

"If it makes any difference to your sense of ethics, it wasn't exactly her idea." Blair pushed back her chair and stood, her breakfast untouched on the table. She stared down at Cam with something close to remorse in her eyes. Nevertheless, her voice was bitter. "And I'm done with her now. It won't happen again."

Without waiting for an answer, the president's daughter turned away abruptly. She didn't so much as glance in Paula Stark's direction.

Cam sat for a moment, watching Blair cross the dining room in angry strides. She struggled for composure, knowing that her anger would only cloud her judgment and make it more difficult for her to do her job. Two of her agents moved quietly from the room to follow Blair at a discreet distance. Cam was confident that they would be ready should the president's daughter decide to leave the lodge. *Let her go and just do the job. Just do the job.*

❖

Half an hour later, Cameron gathered her gear and stepped out into a glorious Colorado morning. The air was crystal clear, the sun on the snow a blazing white glare that forced her to pull on her ski goggles immediately. She knew from communications with the day shift team leader that Blair was on the upper slopes preparing to spend the morning on a long and challenging downhill trail. She skied to the lift to join them.

By the time Cam reached the peak, Blair was about to start her first run down the mountainside. Cam pushed off after her, staying just slightly behind to give Blair plenty of room to maneuver over the steep slope. Content to follow, Cam kept her eyes on Blair's speeding form as she cut a swath through the pristine, snow-covered slopes. She felt only a momentary flicker of surprise when a dark form hurdled from a stand of trees twenty feet from the trail and headed directly for Blair Powell.

Fear was not an emotion that Cam allowed herself. It merely slowed the reflexes and clouded judgment. In the second it took her to reach for her gun, she saw the figure careen into Blair, who went down in a cloud of ice and snow. Instantly, Cam was struck with a sense of déjà vu so sharp that it nearly made her dizzy. The image of Janet falling, an explosion of red on her chest, glided into Cam's mind like a familiar slide on a well-viewed screen. Her stomach clenched as panic threatened to engulf her.

As quickly as the memory formed, Cam forced it away, focusing all of her attention on Blair. The assailant had fallen from the force of the impact and was struggling to rise in the snow a few feet from Blair. Cam skidded to a stop at her side and stepped out of her bindings before she had even stopped moving. She threw herself over Blair's inert body, her gun trained on the figure not far away. With her other hand, she pulled her radio from her belt, shouting hoarsely, "Code red! Code red!"

Even as Cam curled herself protectively around Blair's still form, other agents emerged from the trees on either side, guns drawn, shouting for the assailant to get down. Within seconds, they surrounded him. As soon as Cam was certain that the immediate danger to Blair had passed, she switched radio frequencies and requested urgent transport and a medivac unit to meet them on the slopes. Then, heart pounding triple time, she carefully eased herself off Blair's body. Rapidly, she holstered her Glock and pulled off her gloves.

Jesus, don't let her be hurt badly. Please, please, not her.

Blair lay on her back, eyes closed. She wasn't moving. Her face was pale, so pale.

"Blair, can you hear me?" Gently, Cam pressed two fingers to the carotid artery just below her jaw. The pulse was strong and steady, but she appeared to be unconscious.

"Commander?" a voice from nearby called anxiously.

With fingers that trembled only slightly, Cam opened Blair's parka and slipped her hand inside, searching for evidence of a wound. It was entirely possible that the assailant had slipped a knife or ice pick into her during the collision. She didn't even spare the other agents a glance, but called out, "Get him down the mountain to a secure site. And get me a goddamned medivac unit up here. Now. *Right now."*

One part of her mind worked efficiently, by the book, while another part warred with the terror that threatened to choke her. She slipped her hand under Blair's sweater, finding no evidence of blood. She slid her fingers over the tight abdomen and then tried to check Blair's back without turning her.

"Cam?" Blair whispered groggily. "Cam?"

"Yes." Cam looked down into Blair's unfocused blue eyes, relief surging through her. "Just lie still."

"What…God, my head…what…"

"Everything is all right. You're safe." Carefully, Cam ran her hands along Blair's sides, then onto her chest. Still no sign of a wound. *Thank Christ.*

"What are you doing?"

"Just checking," Cam muttered, her fear subsiding as Blair's voice grew stronger.

"I've been…wanting you to do this, but not…here," Blair commented weakly, a smile flickering uncertainly across her face. She started to push herself up and winced as a barrage of cannon fire began in the back of her head. She fell back limply, groaning faintly.

"Damn it, lie still."

"No choice…what the hell…happened?"

"I don't know yet," Cam said grimly as she zipped up Blair's jacket and then removed her own. Blair was shivering. She spread her jacket over Blair's body. "How do you feel?"

"Keep that on," Blair muttered. "You'll fre…freeze."

"Shut up, Blair," Cam murmured, but she grinned. "What hurts?"

"Just my head." Blair gingerly moved each arm and leg a fraction. Her vision was clearing, and other than a phenomenal headache, she seemed to be fine. "I'm all right."

"We'll have you off the ground in just a minute," Cam said gently. She lifted her radio and barked into it, "Where the hell is medivac?"

Static was all she heard for a moment, and then Mac's voice.

"The helicopter was delayed because of cloud cover. We have an ambulance on its way and there should be snowmobiles on site in approximately two minutes."

"I copy that." Cam didn't like it. It was sloppy work. They should have been informed that the helicopters were unavailable. Nevertheless, at the moment there was nothing she could do.

"I don't want to go to a hospital." Blair reached for Cam's arm, gripping her with surprising strength. "The media will be all over this. My father is in the middle of a summit meeting on disarmament, and there's no need for him to be disturbed."

"It's okay. I'll take care of it." Cam had no intention of arguing with Blair. Even now, her team was taking the suspect downhill to the lodge. She would question him herself as soon as Blair was taken care of. She *had* to approach this as if it were an attempt on Blair's life, because that was all she could assume it was. The time for respecting Blair's wishes was past. This was not something she could compromise about. "Just let me worry about it."

"You're in charge, Commander." Blair watched Cameron's jaw tighten, and she knew there was no room for negotiation. "At least let *me* call him. Tell him I'm all right...before this is all over the news."

"Of course. Just as soon as you're off this mountain." She brushed her hand through Blair's hair. "Now lie still, the stretcher's almost here."

Blair grasped Cam's hand and curled her fingers around Cam's. "Don't leave."

"No," Cam whispered, wanting to take her in her arms but knowing that she couldn't. For so many reasons. She contented herself with hunkering down in the snow as close to her as she could get. "No. No, of course I won't."

❖

Six hours later, Cam nodded to Stark, who was seated outside Blair Powell's hospital room. Stark jumped to her feet.

"Commander."

Cam studied her and the three empty coffee cartons on the floor by her side. Her eyes were over-bright and the tremor in her hands was visible from five feet away. Cam lifted her radio and keyed it. "Mac, send relief for Stark now."

"I'm fine, Commander."

"No, you're not. Get some sleep." Cam ignored the embarrassed blush that followed and gently pushed the door open. She stood for a moment, trying to ascertain in the dim light if Blair was awake.

"Cam?"

"Yes."

"Come in. Leave the light off, though. It tends to make me vomit."

"Roger that." Cam approached the bed and stood looking down at Blair. Still too pale. She had to stifle the urge to reach out and touch her. She tried not to let her worry show. "Did I wake you?"

"No. I was just lying here plotting my escape," Blair said weakly.

Cam laughed with just a hint of sarcasm. "Why is it that I believe you?"

A faint smile flickered across Blair's full lips. For an instant, her eyes sparkled with a youthful joy that had not been present for many years. "Perhaps because you're starting to learn my tricks."

"No." Cam edged a chair close to the side of the bed and sat, leaning forward so that Blair could see her without sitting up. Softly she said, "I doubt very much that I will ever recognize all of your tricks."

"You might," Blair whispered, "if you gave me the chance to teach you."

It was Cam's turn to smile as she chose to ignore the remark. Blair was ill, vulnerable, and this was not the time for them to struggle. "How do you feel?"

"Lousy," Blair answered in an uncharacteristic moment of candor. "I feel like a bus hit me."

"Should I call the nurse? Can I get you anything?" Cam asked. She hated seeing her like this. Her fire and fury were infinitely preferable.

"Your company will do."

Cam stared at Blair's hand lying motionless on the thin hospital-issue covers. She remembered the grace with which that same hand had moved across the sketchpad, capturing her likeness with startling perceptiveness. No one since her mother had been able to portray her so accurately. Without meaning to, she gently covered Blair's slender fingers with her own. She had meant only to reassure her, and found herself reassured instead by the answering press of Blair's fingers slipping through hers.

"Did you speak to your father?"

"Yes. Thank you."

"Good." She was having a hard time sorting out her priorities. For a brief moment on the mountainside, she had thought that Blair was injured, perhaps badly. Her choking fear was much more than just her concern for the person she guarded. She could not bear the thought of Blair being harmed, and she dared not examine too closely the reasons why. She cleared her throat, trying to ignore the sudden tingling in her hand as Blair's fingers intertwined more tightly with hers.

"Your assailant was a sixteen-year-old boy who decided he was going to ski downhill through the trees from an adjoining trail. He wasn't even supposed to be out there, but somehow no one was watching that particular part of the course. He had no idea who you were, and in fact, I still don't think he does."

"So I'm safe for the moment?" Blair asked with just a hint of bitterness.

"This seems unrelated to the events in New York. We've managed to keep this very low profile, and I don't think there's going to be much about it in the media."

Blair sighed gratefully. "Thank you. I want to get out of here this afternoon and go back to the lodge."

"Why does that not surprise me either?" Cam said with resignation. "I've taken the liberty of checking with your physicians, and they told me that if your headache is okay, they'd be willing to discharge you."

"Good. I can handle a headache. I feel like I'm in a fishbowl in here."

"You're sure?" She resisted the urge to brush the errant strands of blond hair off Blair's cheek. "You took a heavy hit out there."

"I've had worse in the ring." Blair tried to sound cavalier but her voice was thin. "I'll take it easy. Just get me out of here. Please."

The plea was so unlike her that Cam's heart twisted in sympathy. She released Blair's hand and stood. "I'll see to the arrangements."

"Thank you."

"No need to thank me," Cam replied, her throat suddenly tight. *You're all right. That's all that matters.*

Cam was almost to the door before Blair spoke.

"And thank you for protecting me this afternoon," she said softly. She still felt the unexpected comfort of Cam's embrace as she had lain in her arms in the snow.

"You don't need to thank me for that either, Ms. Powell." Cam gripped the handle so hard her fingers ached. For a brief moment, she felt again the sheer terror she had experienced as she'd watched Blair fall. She could not afford to feel that for her. She could not afford to feel *anything* for her. In a tone harsher than she intended, she said sharply, "I was only doing my job."

Then she was gone, and Blair was alone once more.

"How's your head?" Cam asked as she slipped into the seat next to Blair. She'd been watching Blair ever since take-off a half-hour before. The blond had grown paler with each passing minute until her face was now chalk-white. Her normally crystal clear blue eyes were dark pools of misery.

"I'll live," Blair responded quietly. In fact, the slightest vertical movement of the aircraft produced a wave of nausea that threatened to overpower her considerable self-control. Fortunately, the skies were clear, and the jet streaked toward New York City with very little turbulence. Otherwise, she was very much afraid she would embarrass herself.

Cam inclined her head closer, although the other agents and Diane were ten rows further forward, engaged in conversation or napping. She and Blair were quite alone. Even so, Cam did not want their private conversation overheard. "You don't have to be a hero, you know. Why don't you take a couple of pain pills and try to rest?"

Blair started to shake her head and abruptly stopped when the slight movement caused her stomach to lurch. "Believe me, Commander, I am no hero. The problem is, the pain pills tend to make me sicker than the pain."

"They affect me that way, too, I'm afraid." Cam shifted in her seat and pushed the center armrest up out of the way, then laid her left arm along the back of the seats. Indicating her shoulder with a tip of her chin, she said softly, "Lean back and close your eyes for the rest of the flight. It's probably the only thing that will do any good. Believe me, I've been in your position more than once. The only way to get through it is pills or sleep."

Blair didn't even have the energy to challenge Cam on the show of friendship, believing the act of kindness to be motivated by sympathy rather than any special feelings for her. Nevertheless, what she needed at that moment was precisely what Cam offered. Simple human comfort.

"Thanks." Moving carefully, Blair allowed herself to relax against Cam's side, resting her head in the curve of Cam's arm. She knew she wouldn't sleep, but perhaps if she closed her eyes the pain would lessen.

"Don't mention it." Gently, Cam stretched her legs out in front of her and settled back into the seat. In only a minute or two, she knew from the rhythmic motion of Blair's chest that she had fallen asleep. The faint background drone of the engines and the warmth of Blair's body along her side lulled her into a sense of peacefulness that she had long forgotten. She stared out the window and thought of nothing. For those few precious hours, Blair's presence was all she needed. As she dozed, she rested her cheek on the fragrant softness of Blair's hair.

❖

As the plane touched down, Cam and Blair awoke together. Neither of them moved. Cam's hand had drifted down from the seat and was curled gently along Blair's side, resting just beneath her breast. In her sleep, Blair had turned to thread her arm around Cam's waist. She lay with her head tucked beneath Cam's chin, resting in her arms. They held each other as if it had always been.

As the others in the cabin began to stand and stretch, Cam lifted her arm from around Blair's body, acutely aware of how much she did not want to let her go. "Ms. Powell, we need to depart."

With a sigh, Blair pushed herself upright and brushed her hands through her wild tresses. She noted with just a hint of surprise that her headache was gone. "Yes, of course we do."

She glanced at Cam, startled to see a fleeting look that might have been regret cross her handsome face. Then, the professional impenetrable mask returned.

"I'll see you on the ground." Rising from her seat, Cam added, "You look better. Feeling all right?"

"Yes, thank you, Commander."

Cam smiled and left her then to move forward and speak to her people regarding the plans for transportation back to the apartment. Diane worked her way down the aisle to Cam's vacant seat.

"You two looked very cozy together," she remarked dryly.

"Leave it alone, Diane," Blair said quietly.

Diane bit back the retort she had been about to make. There was something in her old friend's voice that warned her off. In fact, they *had* looked very good together. *Too* good together. They looked as if they had held each other a thousand times before. Diane simply shook her head and left unspoken her words of caution. Something told her that Blair was beyond hearing.

CHAPTER ELEVEN

Cameron set down her paper cup of coffee on the worktable and glanced over at Mac with a quizzical lift of her eyebrow. "Is she still upstairs?"

"Yup, three days straight," Mac said, shaking his head. "Still no briefing?"

"No. Just a message that she had no plans." Cam wasn't sure what to make of it, but she knew she didn't like it. Ever since they had touched down at Triboro, Blair had not been herself. She had sent word that she intended to work in her studio and would not require daily meetings with Cam. Cam had not protested, feeling that to do so would be a further invasion of Blair's privacy. Nevertheless, the atmosphere in the command center resembled the calm before the storm. All of them expected Blair to burst forth from her isolation at any moment and lead them once again on a merry chase. For her part, Cam almost wished she would. There was something unnerving about the sudden change in Blair's behavior.

"Better the enemy I know," Cam muttered in a rare display of irritation. She picked up her coffee and headed to her small glass-enclosed office. Mac looked after her, thinking that Blair Powell wasn't the only one who was not acting like herself.

As the week progressed without change, waiting became the new routine. Shifts changed, agents came and went. Those on site whiled away the hours reading, playing cards, and generally wondering when the bomb would drop. Cam spent as little time as possible within the confines of the command center. She jogged, she worked out, she read in her apartment. She left strict orders to be called the moment Blair gave any indication that she was preparing to leave the building and tried not to think about how much she missed seeing her every day. Eight nights after their return from Colorado, the call finally came.

"Egret is flying," Mac informed her.

"What? *Alone?* "

"Yes, ma'am. She just got into a cab and is headed downtown."

"God damn it," Cam cursed. "How did you let that happen?"

"There wasn't anything we could do short of physically stopping her." Mac's discomfort was apparent, even over the phone. "She just walked out of the building without warning, stepped into the street, and flagged down a Checker. We were lucky to get the car out fast enough to follow her."

Cam sighed slightly in relief. "Then you have a location for her?"

"Roger that. Hold on a second."

Cam paced the confines of her living room, the cellular phone gripped tightly in her hand. Although they had had no further contact from whoever had left the note outside Blair's door, she was worried that they weren't the only ones watching the president's daughter. Anytime Blair was without an escort, Cam was fearful for her safety.

"She just went into a bar on Houston," Mac informed her.

"Name and address?" Cam asked tersely.

"Rendezvous," Mac stated. After a second, he gave her the address as well.

"Hold a team outside with the vehicle. I'm on my way."

Less than fifteen minutes later, Cam entered the bar, scanning the already crowded dance floor and surrounding tables for Blair. It was approaching midnight on a Saturday night, and the room was packed. The lighting was dim and the air thick with smoke, making it difficult for her to see across the room. She threaded her way through the clusters of people at the perimeter of the room, guessing that Blair would be in the shadows somewhere. Sure enough, she finally saw her talking to a young woman with impressive tattoos encircling both upper arms.

The woman with Blair was obviously a serious body-builder. Her tight white tank top was clearly meant to display her hard-earned physique, and her low-cut button-fly jeans showed off her muscular thighs to full advantage. At the moment, her hand was stroking the length of Blair's bare arm, drawing closer to Blair's breast with each movement. Cam gritted her teeth and tried to ignore the seduction in progress. Watching as Blair pressed closer to the other woman, she remembered the brief moment when Blair had moved against her like that, claiming her effortlessly with a kiss. Cam's body immediately stirred to the memory, her clitoris hardening almost instantly.

Jesus Christ, what the hell is the matter with you?

Cam forced herself to ignore the throbbing between her thighs. Nevertheless, she found herself averting her gaze when Blair cupped the woman's face in her hand and licked slowly along the edge of her jaw, finally thrusting her tongue between the parted lips. That was the moment when Cam finally admitted to herself that she couldn't do what she had come there to do. She couldn't watch Blair touch another woman, and if she couldn't, she couldn't protect her either. Anger surged through her as she spoke harshly into her wrist microphone.

"I want the first team in here *now* to take over this surveillance." She abruptly turned her back as the two women began to kiss ferociously, their hands roaming over each other with abandon. As soon as she saw Stark and Grant enter the bar, she pushed her way through the crowd and out onto the street. She crossed quickly to the second car and radioed headquarters.

"Mac, I want you to take over for me for the next twelve hours. If there's an emergency, page me. Otherwise, I'm unavailable." She didn't wait for his reply but rapped sharply on the glass partition to get Taylor's attention. "Take me to the airport."

As she waited in a terminal for her flight, she dialed a familiar number in Washington, D.C. and arranged for the only hope she had of driving Blair from her consciousness.

❖

"Ah, God...I can't," Cam gasped hoarsely. "I'm sorry...I want to. I just...can't."

The blond raised her head, gazing up the long expanse of Cam's torso. "That's not what your body is telling me."

"Tired," Cam sighed, weary in so much more than body. "Too tired."

"You don't have to do anything." Claire rested her cheek against Cam's thigh, one hand softly stroking between Cam's legs. "Besides, I'm not done yet."

"I think *I* am. It's not your fault." Cam gently insinuated her fingers into the hair at the back of her visitor's neck. She tugged lightly. "Come lie beside me."

Claire slipped from between Cam's legs and moved up to recline against her body, resting her head on Cam's shoulder. Her hand lay on Cam's stomach, stroking in easy circles. They had very rarely been together this way, so close, for so long. There was an intimacy that was new; wonderful and frightening at the same time. The boundaries between business and affection had blurred for her some time ago, but until now, she'd had it under control. Something had changed, and it appeared to be her dark-haired client. Some barrier had fallen, leaving the formerly guarded woman open, more exposed. Even more desirable, if that were possible. Claire pressed her lips to Cam's shoulder. "Let me. You need this."

"No." Cam shifted slightly, brushing a kiss across Claire's forehead. Softly, she said, "Let me make love to *you.*"

"That's not what this is about," Claire protested gently, fearing the regret that would follow, perhaps for both of them. "I don't need you to do that."

"*I* need to," Cam insisted. It was the first time she had ever suggested it. She wanted to touch someone, needed to see if she still could. "After all this time, I want to give you something back."

"Just hold me," Claire requested, hearing what Cam wasn't saying. She knew that Cam wanted more than to thank her; she wanted to say goodbye, whether she knew it or not. Over the years, there had been many goodbyes. This was the one that was going to be the hardest. "Hold me. That's all I need."

"I can do that," Cam murmured, her lips against Claire's temple. She cradled the other woman closer, closed her eyes, and tried to empty her mind. Tried not to think about her anger and confusion every time she imagined Blair making love to yet another stranger. Tried to ignore the jealousy, knowing that she had no right to it. Tried to ignore the simple fact that she wanted it to be her that Blair was caressing, wanted it to be Blair next to her in the night. She sighed, tracing her fingertips over Claire's arm as she drifted.

Claire listened to the steady heartbeat beneath her cheek as she ran her fingers lightly over Cam's flushed skin. Gently, she traced the outline of her ribs and hip, stroked the soft curve of the underside of her breasts, smoothed the flat of her hand over the taut muscles of her stomach. She didn't hurry. There was no end except the dawn.

Slowly, Cam relaxed under the undemanding touch. Eventually, her thoughts were eclipsed by an awareness of her body's response to Claire's attention. Her skin began to tingle, her leg muscles tightened, and her hips rolled gently with each subtle stroke. Her clitoris once again swelled in anticipation. This time, the urgency was gone, and she allowed herself the luxury of simply accepting the pleasure. Her mind collapsed into a single point of sensation, centered within the pulsating pressure between her legs.

"Ahh...that's good."

"Yes."

Groaning faintly, she lifted her pelvis higher, silently urging Claire's hand lower. Her breath escaped on a sigh as two fingers enclosed the shaft of her clitoris, milking slowly along its length. Wetness spread along the inside of her thighs, and when one soft stroke brushed the warm moisture over the prominence of exposed nerves, she moaned again.

"God, that makes me want to come," she murmured breathlessly.

"Don't rush," Claire whispered softly. She slipped fingers inside, then back out and upward, a steady rhythm that matched Cam's unconscious movements. She sensed the building pressure and felt the tender tissues beneath her fingertips thicken even more, swelling to the point of explosion.

"I want to come." Urgent now.

"Yes. Soon."

Cam gripped the sheets convulsively in her left hand, her right arm holding Claire tightly. She turned her face against the sweet comfort of Claire's skin and allowed her body to surrender to the inevitable. As her stomach clenched and a hoarse cry was wrenched from her depths, Blair Powell's face flickered across the inner surface of her eyelids.

❖

Three hundred miles away, Blair stood in a studio apartment on the fourth floor of a building in Greenwich Village that had seen better days. She casually studied the clothes hanging on a rack that had been pushed into the corner, seeming to have forgotten the woman who had brought her there.

"Nice collection of ties you have here," Blair commented as she fingered the lengths of silk and cotton draped over a hanger at the end of the rack. Without looking at the other woman, she continued, "Let's see what kind of use we can put these to. Why don't you take your clothes off and lie face down on the bed."

"What?" The young butch stared at her in amazement. Clearly, Blair's collar-length blond hair, make-up, and braless breasts beneath the tight white T-shirt did not necessarily spell "femme."

"You heard me," Blair remarked as she turned with a handful of wide silk ties in her hand. "Now do it."

As much as she hated to relinquish her self-assumed dominance, Blair's partner was intrigued and more than a little excited by the commanding tone in Blair's voice. Trying to maintain her façade of nonchalance, the dark-haired body-builder removed her leather and denim, pulled off her briefs, and shed her boots and socks. Naked, and feeling more than a little uncertain, she lay face down on her own bed, welcoming the pillow that allowed her to hide her face.

"Better." Blair crossed to her side and slipped a loop fashioned from one of the ties around the woman's right wrist. She ran the length of fabric over the edge of the sofa bed and around the frame, then quickly followed suit with the other wrist and both ankles. Once the woman was totally immobilized, she removed the pillow.

"I want you to be able to breathe. But keep your eyes closed."

Blair stepped back, lit several candles she had noticed on the windowsill, and placed them on the small end table. In the flickering candlelight, she studied the woman's body. She was beautiful. Smooth, tight skin the color of light cocoa; muscles rippling under the sweat-slick surface; thick lustrous hair just beginning to curl at the base of her neck. Her face in profile was sharply defined and arrogant even in repose. Altogether, she was a fine specimen of young butch sexuality.

Still, Blair had to struggle not to compare her form to the long, lean lines of Cam's body. She did not want to remember the alluring maturity etched into Cam's elegant features, or the smoldering sensuality in her dark eyes, or the aching softness of her full lips. For the last week she'd tried everything she knew to forget the plane ride and Cam's arms around her—hours upon hours of work, secluded in her loft. It hadn't worked. The only way she could hope to drive Cam from her awareness was to fill her senses with the sight, and the sound, and the feel of another woman.

"Lie still."

Still fully clothed, Blair climbed onto the bed and stretched out on top of the restrained woman. She ran her fingers over the surface of the bound arms, tasted the salt at the base of her neck, sucked an earlobe into her mouth. Dimly, she heard a groan as she captured the soft skin along the jaw between her teeth, tugging lightly, quickly erasing the pinpoints of pain with a kiss.

"No," Blair breathed when her captive struggled to turn her face, desperately seeking Blair's lips. Sitting up slightly, Blair traced the muscles of the other woman's shoulders and back and flanks, ending at her well-formed buttocks. Moving down the bed, she kneaded the thick gluteal muscles, pushing and separating them, exposing the cleft between them to her view. She traced the puckered muscle, then pressed lightly.

"Oh, please," the young stranger moaned, an edge of fear in her voice.

"Quiet," Blair said softly. "I won't hurt you."

She knelt between the strong, now quivering thighs and circled the sensitive tissues with a moistened fingertip. The tight sphincter spasmed as she softly stroked the outer rim.

"Oh God." No fear now. Need.

Blair ran her tongue between the woman's splayed thighs, tasting for the first time the thick, heady juices of her young lover's desire. She licked lightly over the swollen folds, traced the furrows with her tongue, kissed the thickening clitoris, moving tantalizingly from one spot to the next.

"If you…oh, you'll make me come," gasped the young woman.

"Soon," Blair murmured.

"Want to now…so bad."

Blair lost herself in the sensations—in the intoxicating smell, the incredible softness, the welcoming heat. This was woman, any woman, *every* woman. As she pressed her face deeper, immersing herself, she felt her lover's impending orgasm flutter between her lips. Quickly, she stretched out full-length on the bed and encircled the woman's waist, frantically caressing the engorged tissues with her lips and tongue. As the body beneath her convulsed amidst sobs and cries and choked moans, Blair squeezed her eyes tightly closed, wanting to know only this incredible moment of intense connection. But even with the woman climaxing in her mouth, Blair couldn't help but wish that it were Cameron Roberts surrendering to her touch.

❖

Cam rolled over and fumbled for the phone on the bedside table. The digital clock read 4:45. She was disoriented as to where she was and exactly what time it was. The bed beside her was empty, but there was a lingering warmth that suggested it had recently been occupied. As the phone rang insistently, her eyes adjusted to the dark and she recognized her own bedroom in Washington, D.C. As she lifted the receiver, her mind registered her recent flight from New York and her frantic attempts to forget Blair Powell in the embrace of another woman.

"Roberts," she growled, trying to ignore the unsettling thoughts.

"It's Mac, Commander. I'm sorry to disturb you, but I thought you would want to know—"

Cam sat up abruptly in bed, her mind crystal clear, but her heart pounding. "Egret? Is she secure?"

"Yes, ma'am," Mac hurried to assure her. "We have her under constant surveillance, and we know exactly where she is. But we just received another contact from Loverboy."

That was the name the security team had given the UNSUB—unidentified subject—who had left the note at Blair's door.

"What is it?" Cam queried as she swung out of bed and began searching the room for her clothes. She noticed a folded sheet of notepaper on her dressing table and slipped it into the pocket of her trousers.

"Photographs," Mac said grimly. "There's a very good close-up of Egret leaving the apartment building last night. Infrared—professional quality."

"Son of a bitch. That means he's been watching the building from somewhere close by. How did you get them?" Phone under her chin, Cam hastily buttoned her shirt, then threaded a narrow leather belt through the loops of her pants. A second later she had found one shoe and was peering under the bed for the other.

"Taylor noticed a manila envelope propped up against the counter in the lobby when he came on for the night shift. It had Egret's name on it."

Cam stopped abruptly in the middle of the floor, a shoe in one hand, her portable phone in the other. She felt a brief thrill of elation. "Then we've got him! There are video cameras all over that lobby as well as at the entrance. We *must* have an image of him. I want all of the tapes brought up to the command center for review. Also, run a check on the license plates of every car parked around the park right now. Then contact the cab companies for all fares in the last twenty-four hours to within a ten-block radius of Egret's address."

"That's a lot of legwork, Commander," Mac said doubtfully.

"See that it's done," she barked.

"Yes, ma'am!"

"I'll catch the next commuter flight. Assemble the entire team, day and night shifts, at 0700."

"Roger that."

"And Mac," Cam continued in a quieter voice. "Get Egret back to her apartment."

There was a beat of silence over the line. Mac cleared his throat, choosing his words carefully. He wasn't sure why, but he felt uncomfortable delivering the next information. "Uh, Commander—at the moment, Egret is with an unidentified female, who almost certainly does not know Egret's identity. If we roust her, there is no way we'll be able to guarantee silence regarding her identity."

Cam flashed back to the young woman Blair had been fondling in the bar. Of course Blair would have gone home with her. And why not? The stranger was just the kind of conquest Blair would thrill to.

"Then I want her in a car the minute she steps out onto the sidewalk. And Mac—if anyone loses her, it's their job."

"I guarantee I will have her back here ASAP." As he hung up the phone, he said a fervent prayer that he could deliver on his promise.

CHAPTER TWELVE

At 0659, Cam walked into the command center and strode to the head of the table where the entire team was gathered. Despite her lack of sleep, she looked focused and intent. Without preamble, she said, "Let's have the analysis on the photograph."

Jeremy Finch, a short, mildly overweight, bespectacled agent, cleared his throat. He was the resident nerd—the computer genius and technical wizard. "We've analyzed the potential elevation and angle of view by extrapolating from the available shadows and the estimated time of day."

"Cut to the chase, Agent," Cam snapped with a rare show of impatience.

"Uh, basically, the photograph was taken from one of the buildings facing Egret's across Gramercy Park." He looked down at the tabletop uncomfortably.

"The *rooftop?*"

"Not necessarily, Commander." Finch blinked rapidly behind his glasses. "Height projections suggest anywhere above eighty feet."

"That leaves us with a lot of potential sites, Agent Finch." Cam stared at him, biting back another sarcastic remark. It wasn't his fault that he couldn't manufacture evidence.

"Yes, ma'am, I know that." Finch nodded almost miserably. Like every other agent in the room, he had come to value his position on this team and felt a sense of loyalty to his intense, demanding commander. "What it *does* tell us is that the shooter has a fixed location, rather than a vehicle. Therefore, there is a better chance of finding him, since he may be relatively stationary."

"You're right." She took a minute to settle herself. Her impatience was born of fear, and she needed to curb both emotions.

Blair Powell would not be harmed. Not now. Not ever. "Okay—I want a list of every occupant of every building on *each* side of the square, not just the street directly across from this building. He could live in one place and be using a different locale for his surveillance. You'll need to check realtors, building managers, and also any corporations which lease apartments for use by employees. It's possible that our UNSUB is only here intermittently when business demands it."

"We have people assigned to begin the reconnaissance at the opening of business hours," Mac interjected.

"Fine. Finch, pull all the tapes from last night. Let's see if we can spot the drop."

They spent a few moments reviewing other methods of narrowing down the list of potential perpetrators who might have access to the surrounding buildings. Cam outlined the change in coverage that would be required now that the threat status had been upgraded. Finally, she looked around the table, meeting the eyes of each of her agents.

"I'm going to have to report this to the White House. At this point, we must assume that Blair Powell is in imminent danger of either an assassination or abduction attempt. I'm going to recommend that she be secluded until such time as we deem the threat neutralized. It is possible—actually *probable*—that this investigation will be removed from our jurisdiction—" She held up her hand for silence as the agents shifted in their seats and murmured in protest.

"I know how you feel, and I think that we are the best people to protect her *as well as* to get to the bottom of this. But situations like this often become political, and it's possible we will have nothing to say about it. If it comes to that, I expect total cooperation with whoever is running the investigation. Remember, the bottom line is Egret's safety. There is no room for ego or personal gain where she is concerned."

She waited a beat. "Am I clear on that?"

A chorus of *Yes, ma'ams* followed.

"Good. Let's get to work. Mac, a moment, please." Cam turned to him as the others filed out. "As soon as Ms. Powell arrives home, inform me. I'll meet with her and advise her of the situation. That's all."

Mac merely nodded. Today was not a day to do anything but follow orders. The Commander was on fire.

❖

Cam stalked through the command center to the elevators and left the building without speaking to anyone. She crossed the square to her own apartment and shed her clothes immediately upon entering. She went to the bathroom and stepped into the shower, then turned the cold water on full and let it blast the fatigue from her body and her mind. She was furious. Furious that someone dared threaten Blair Powell for no other reason than the position she represented. She was furious at herself for allowing her feelings for Blair to interfere with her duty. She was furious that the thought of any harm coming to Blair terrified her.

When the phone rang two hours later and Mac notified her that Blair had returned to her penthouse apartment, Cam was seated in front of her large bay windows, dressed in a starched white shirt, black silk trousers, and a charcoal gray silk jacket. She had been waiting for the call, her mind uncommonly still. She felt sure of herself for the first time in weeks.

❖

"What's the emergency?" Blair asked more abruptly than she had intended. She stood across the room from Cam in just her robe, having barely gotten out of the shower when she had been informed that her security chief was on her way up. "This isn't a very good time. Can't we do this later?"

She had not seen Cam in almost ten days. Since returning from the ski resort, she had worked feverishly, spending long hours applying paint to canvas, creating sweeping abstract vistas of anger and longing and frustrated desire. When finally her emotions had run dry, she'd looked up from her easel and felt the walls of her loft closing in on her. Cam's unbidden image still haunted her. The comfort of Cam's embrace on the airplane had been harder to forget than the sexual desire that had plagued her previously. Lust was something she could control, ignoring it, or, if necessary, sating it elsewhere. What she felt for Cameron Roberts was something she hadn't experienced since she had been innocent enough to believe in love. More than anything else, it frightened her.

"What is it?" Blair asked quietly when she got no answer. Cam, normally so imperturbable, looked tense, and her eyes were deeply shadowed with fatigue. Blair's heart twisted suddenly. "My father?"

"No," Cam said quickly. "No, I'm sorry. He's fine."

"Then what?"

"There's been further contact from the stalker," Cam said flatly. "A photograph was left sometime last night."

"Of me?" Blair shivered inwardly, her stomach churning at the thought.

"Yes. It was taken when you left the building last night."

"My god," she exclaimed, thinking of the apartment she'd just left. Of an unsuspecting woman still asleep in the tangled sheets. "Was I followed? Cam, there's a woman—"

Cam shook her head, careful to keep her expression blank. "We don't have any reason to think she's in danger. The apartment where you spent the night was under surveillance the entire time."

"Where did they pick me up?"

"From here." Cam smiled grimly. "We got lucky for once and trailed your cab."

Blair studied Cam's face. "Who was in the bar?"

"First me, then Stark."

"I didn't see you."

"No, I wouldn't imagine so."

"Cam," Blair's tone was quiet, her eyes dark. *I didn't mean for you to see that. I just wanted to…not want you for a few hours.*

Cam made an impatient gesture with her hand. She couldn't let her feelings about Blair's sexual foray distract her. Especially not now. "That doesn't matter. What matters is the situation with this UNSUB."

"Which is what, exactly?" Blair asked pointedly, aware that Cam had cut off any further discussion of the personal.

"The photographs may be nothing more than his way of letting us know that he's around—empty posturing. But it may also be an indication that he's escalating. I have to assume that to be true."

Blair took a deep breath. "What do you intend to do about it?"

"I thought it only right to inform you first that I am flying to Washington later this morning to conference with my assistant director and probably the chief of staff. I would anticipate that a task force will be formed to investigate and apprehend this individual."

Blair said nothing, turning to look out her windows into the park below. She thought she knew how a caged animal felt. "What will that mean for me?"

Cameron saw the rigid set of her back and heard the slight tremor in her voice. For an instant, she wanted to take Blair into her arms and comfort her. Instead, she forced herself to say, "I would imagine you'll be moved out of the city until he's in custody."

Blair spun around, her blue eyes nearly purple with fury. "You mean they'll close me up in some compound with guards twenty-four hours a day, as if my life were so insignificant I could walk away and leave everything behind."

"No." Cam took a step forward, then stopped herself. Forcing herself to be calm, she said firmly, "As if your life were too important to risk for a single moment."

"Bullshit!" Blair spat. "The only thing you people care about is protecting the reputation of the United States government and the people who run it."

"Blair—"

"Don't, Cam. At least don't lie to me." Blair turned on her heel and stalked to the opposite side of the room, stepping behind the partition that enclosed her sleeping area.

After a moment, Cam followed. Blair was hastily throwing clothes into a suitcase.

"Exactly what do you think you're doing?" Cam's tone was lethally cold.

Blair didn't bother to look up. She dropped the robe onto the floor, naked beneath. She stepped into jeans, pulled a sweater over her head, and shoved bare feet into loafers. Silently, she paced to the dresser and searched hastily for her wallet and keys. When she finally looked at Cam, her face was set.

"I'm getting out of here. I wouldn't suggest you try to stop me. I don't think my father would be pleased if I was manhandled by one of his Secret Service agents." Then she reached for her bag and was stunned when Cam grasped her forcibly by the shoulders, stopping her in her tracks.

"I don't give a *fuck* what your father thinks!" Cam seethed. "I don't even give a fuck what *you* think. You are *not* leaving this apartment."

For a brief second, Cam became every person who had ever conspired to keep Blair a captive in a life she had never chosen. Dropping the keys, she swung her hand at Cam's face, lashing out not at the woman who had done nothing more than attempt to protect her, but at the faceless many that had carried out their orders despite her wishes.

Reflexively, Cam intercepted the blow with her left arm, angry not at Blair for attempting to strike her, but at Blair's stubborn refusal to accept that she was in danger. Then, Cam's fear surfaced on a wave of uncontrollable desire, and she pulled Blair into her arms. Covering Blair's mouth with her own, Cam kissed her roughly, her hands pinning Blair's arms to her sides as she pulled the unsuspecting woman hard into her embrace.

For a moment, Blair was too shocked to react, but there was never an instant of resistance. When she felt Cam's mouth on hers, she kissed her back, her tongue searching urgently to join Cam's, her arms tight around Cam's waist as their legs entwined.

Cam's breath rasped in her chest as reason all but deserted her. She had wanted Blair so badly, for what seemed like forever, and her body rapidly raced out of control. She groaned, burying her face against Blair's neck as she pushed one hand beneath the sweater, finding flesh.

Blair arched her pelvis into Cam and tilted her head back, exposing her neck as if for sacrifice. "Oh God, Cam, God, yes… touch me."

The sound of Blair's voice sliced through Cam's consciousness, paralyzing her as awareness crashed upon her. *My god, what am I doing!*

Cam halted her feverish caresses, but did not let go of the woman in her arms. Instead, she cradled her closer, pressing her lips to Blair's ear. Shuddering with arousal, she whispered urgently, "I'm sorry, I'm sorry. Forgive me."

"No!" Blair choked, fisting one hand in Cam's hair, forcing her head back. "Look at me."

Groaning, nearly mad, Cam fell into Blair's eyes.

"Touch me," Blair whispered into Cam's soul. "I need you."

"I can't," Cam murmured in anguish. She couldn't do this, not again. She couldn't feel this much, she couldn't *want* this much. She had not touched another woman with passion since the morning she had last made love to Janet. Six hours later she had held her helplessly as she lay dying. She had vowed never to feel the longing, or the loss, again. "God, I can't."

"No, of course you can't." Blair pushed away from her unsteadily, running her trembling hands through her hair. Her eyes were bruised, from passion and from the pain of Cam's rejection. "It's not in your job description, is it, Commander? You can't feel anything for me because it would interfere with your duty. Isn't that right?"

Cam shook so badly she wasn't sure she could stay standing, but she willed her voice to be firm. "When I meet with the assistant director in Washington, I'm going to resign this command. Whatever you may think of me, I will not jeopardize your safety by remaining. I *can't* do my duty, simply because I can't think of you as just another assignment."

When Cam turned to leave, Blair called, "Wait!"

The nearly helpless note in her voice caused Cam to stop. Hoarsely, she asked, "What?"

"I *have* to attend the opening of the new children's wing at the city hospital this afternoon at one. It's been arranged for months, and there are children who might not...be there...later." Blair wanted to touch her, just for the comfort of it, but she didn't dare move. "Can't all of this wait until after that?"

Cam nodded slowly, knowing if she turned around she'd reach for her again. "I'll arrange to leave for Washington immediately after that."

"Thank you," Blair whispered as Cam walked away.

❖

At 12:30 that afternoon, Cam stood outside Blair's door, dressed much the same as she had been that morning. She had changed shirts, substituting a pale gray silk for the white. When she knocked, Blair opened her apartment door immediately. She wore a simple black sheath accented by a string of gray pearls at her neck. Her low heels brought her to exactly Cam's height. Anyone seeing them together would have thought they made a striking couple.

"Will you come inside the hospital with me?" Blair asked, her eyes meeting Cam's in an unusual display of vulnerability. "Ever since my mother…I hate hospitals."

"Yes. Every step," Cam said quietly, knowing how hard this visit must be for her.

"I…appreciate it," Blair whispered.

As Blair stepped to Cam's side, Cam softly touched her hand. "It will be all right."

Three other agents joined them as they exited the elevator and walked toward the lobby doors. Mac had the Suburban waiting at the curb, the rear doors open and the engine running. The bright afternoon sunlight outside the large glass doors cast a blinding glare directly into their faces. Stark and Fielding exited first, followed by Cam and Grant, Blair between them. Automatically, Cam looked up, squinting into the sun, scanning the buildings across the small square. She sensed rather than saw movement flickering somewhere in the haze that silhouetted the ornate cornices along the rooftops.

Cameron Roberts's instincts were her guiding force, the one thing in her life she neither questioned nor doubted. She stepped quickly in front of Blair, pushing her backwards into the shelter of the entrance. Then, she must have tripped, because the next thing she knew, she was kneeling on the sidewalk, trying to catch her breath. A cacophony of cries filled her head as agents screamed into their mikes.

Code red, code red…Oh fuck fuck fuck…

"Get…her…inside," Cam ordered, but her voice came out a whisper on a plume of red mist. She had her gun in her right hand, but it was very difficult to raise her arm. With huge effort, she turned her head, searching for Blair. Though her vision was oddly blurred, she saw Blair surrounded by agents, who were half carrying her back into the building. Blair appeared to be struggling, her hand outstretched toward Cam. Someone far away screamed Cam's name, an agonized, animal howl of pain. Then—silence.

She's safe.

Cam's mind was quite clear. Blair was safe, and her duty was done. Accepting the strange lassitude that suffused her, she sank slowly onto her back. Then she opened her hand and let her gun rest gently on the sidewalk. Staring up into the bluest sky she could ever recall, Cam peacefully closed her eyes as her heart ceased to beat.

CHAPTER THIRTEEN

Mac came crashing through the double glass doors just as Blair broke Stark's hold. Shouldering past a stunned Taylor, Blair raced across the lobby toward the entrance. She'd almost made it back outside when Mac caught her from behind, wrapped both arms around her, and pulled her back. "Ms. Powell, no!"

"Let me go," Blair screamed. She looked beyond him and saw Cam fall, then lie still. So terribly still. The pool of blood on the sidewalk beneath her was bright red. And enormous. Somewhere close by, sirens sounded. "Oh my god. Oh my god. She's out there alone! Let me go!"

"The EMTs are almost here." He had to get her upstairs, out of the potential line of fire. "Stark, key the elevator!"

Blair thought her head would explode. All she wanted was to get to Cam. She was an experienced fighter, and swiftly, she brought one elbow hard into his solar plexus. The air rushed from his chest, and he loosened his hold. She wrenched free only to be picked up bodily by the other three agents and carried across the lobby and into the elevator.

"Get her to the command center," Mac called as the doors slid closed.

"Let me go." Blair's voice was steady and so firm that the three agents did as they were told, dropping their hands and stepping back from her.

Stark, white-faced, with the barest hint of a tremor in her voice, asked, "Are you hurt?"

"No." Blair swayed slightly as the elevator glided to a halt on the eighth floor. When the doors open, they all stood still for a moment, shell-shocked.

Again, it was Stark who took charge. "Come this way, please, Ms. Powell."

"Yes," Blair replied, stepping out blindly, unable to see anything except Cam on the ground. She blinked in the harsh glare of the overhead lights and glanced around the room. She'd been there before, but not often. It looked like any large office, with the exception of the bank of wide-screen monitors that took up most of one end of the room. Automatically, she moved toward them. It took her only an instant to find the one displaying the image from the camera over the entrance to her apartment building. She placed both hands on top of the workstation counter and leaned close, trying to make sense of what she was seeing.

Two people, EMTs it appeared, were working on Cam, one astride her body, pumping rhythmically on her chest, the other pushing tubes into her arms. Police in combat gear crowded around. Mac was kneeling on the sidewalk by her side.

"Ms. Powell," Stark said softly in her ear. "I don't think—"

"Can you make this image larger?" Blair asked without turning from the screen.

"I...I don't—"

"Please, Paula." Blair's voice was quietly urgent. "I want to see her face."

"Yes, ma'am." Stark reached down to the keyboard and adjusted the angle of view and the zoom. The commander's eyes were closed, and she might have been asleep except for the slight trickle of blood at the corner of her mouth.

"Can you get audio?" Blair whispered hoarsely, resting her fingertips on the surface of the monitor, just touching Cam's cheek. *Cam. Oh God. This can't be happening.*

"No, I'm sorry." Stark was very much afraid she was going to cry, and she bit the inside of her lip to take her mind off the terrible scene on the screen and the agonizing sight of Blair Powell watching.

"I want to go to the hospital," Blair murmured, never taking her eyes away as the stretcher came into view and Cam's body was rapidly shifted onto it. When she could no longer see her, she straightened, shivering, although she didn't think she was cold. "Now, please."

"That won't be possible," Stark said as gently as she could, although her tone left no room for negotiation. She expected to get a call from Mac, or someone, any second directing them to evacuate to a safe house. She was a bit surprised that the SWAT team hadn't made it upstairs.

Blair turned to her then, her blue eyes as brilliantly cold as winter snow. "I will go with or without you, Agent Stark. Your choice."

With that she walked away, leaving Stark to shout into her wrist mike the one phrase guaranteed to mobilize the entire team.

"Egret is flying."

❖

Mac crowded into the back of the ambulance, wanting desperately to contact Stark but unsure of the security of their long-distance com links. He watched the continued resuscitation, his stomach in knots. *At least Egret is secure. Stark knows the drill. Christ, why can't they move a little faster?*

It took forever to get to the hospital fifteen blocks away.

"You'll have to wait outside, sir."

"Look," he held up his ID to the dark-haired woman in the navy blue scrubs, "I'm not leaving her."

The harried surgeon frowned. "Stay out of the way, then."

"Roger that," he muttered, craning his neck to see what was happening beyond the edge of the white curtain. Controlled chaos was what it looked like. Or maybe just chaos. The commander was surrounded by people, all of them doing something to her. The female EMT still straddled her chest, arms rhythmically pumping, counting with the steady cadence of a metronome.

One, two, three, four...breath...One two three four...breath...

They'd cut most of her clothes off. There was a hole above her left breast and a hell of a lot of blood.

We need another line here...Hang more fluid...Son of a bitch!...I can't get a blood pressure...Where the fuck is the O neg?

He watched the monitors and what he saw made his guts churn. There wasn't anything on them.

Push the intracardiac epi again... Anything?...crack her chest...

The surgeon, the cool-eyed tall one, held out her hand. A nurse put a scalpel in it.

Here we go...I've got a rhythm...shit, still no pulse...keep up the compression...nothing...pump more blood...

Mac avoided looking at the woman's hands inside the commander's chest. He watched the flat green line race across the screen, then felt his heart stutter when a single blip became several, and finally a steady line of them. His knees were suddenly weak. *Oh, thank Christ.*

The surgeon halted, stared at the pressure readout with an expression that would have been frightening if she'd had a gun in her hand. She looked as if she were in the middle of a battle.

Come on, come on...yeah, there she goes... Tell the OR we're coming up... move it...

Mac sagged in relief as the entire entourage barreled by him, and after taking a second to catch his breath, he followed. One step into the waiting room and he stopped dead in his tracks, staring in disbelief. *Tell me I'm not seeing this.*

❖

"How is she?" Blair demanded as she strode across the room toward Mac with Stark and Grant flanking her. "Can I see her?"

Stunned, diplomacy forgotten, Mac snapped, "This area is not secure. You *cannot* be here."

"I'm here. I'm not leaving." Blair took a deep breath. *Cooperate. I promised Cam I'd cooperate. Oh, Cam. Please. It can't end like this.* "Do what you have to do, Agent Phillips, but I'm not leaving until she's out of danger. Put a dozen agents on me—I don't care."

He looked past her out the emergency entrance as another Suburban squealed to a halt and the rest of the team piled out. "The six of us will do for now. Let's find someplace more private than this."

"Thank you, Mac," Blair said softly. "Please...tell me how she is."

As they walked down the now eerily deserted corridor toward a small lounge, he replied, "They just took her to the operating room."

"Was she conscious?" The image of Cam lying so still wouldn't leave her mind.

Mac cleared his throat. "Ms. Powell—"

"Just say it, Mac. Please."

"She arrived here with no vital signs—" He clenched his jaw at the small moan, quickly stifled, from the woman beside him. Hurriedly, he added, "But they'd been doing CPR in the field. They got her back."

They got her back. Where had she gone? Could it really all end so quickly? Of course it can. She'd just touched my hand, said it would be all right. She stepped in front of me. Oh my god, she stepped in front of me.

"Excuse me," Blair said abruptly as she turned aside and disappeared into a restroom.

"Stark," Mac snapped. "Go."

"Yes, sir."

Stark found her braced over a sink, her hands curled around the edges of the white porcelain, her breath coming in quick, short gasps. Protocol dictated that Stark just guard her, not comfort her, but she couldn't forget how the president's daughter had looked watching the monitor, trying to touch the fallen commander through the screen. *Jesus, ten days ago she held me...*

Tentatively, Stark placed her fingertips on Blair's shoulder. She couldn't see her face, but she could feel her shake. "Ms. Powell—"

"I'm all right," Blair said faintly, keeping her head turned away. "I just need...a minute."

"Of course." Stark dropped her hand and stepped back, but she stayed close.

Blair closed her eyes and willed her stomach to settle. Tried to will away the horrible realization that another human being had almost died in her place. A woman she lov—

That can't be. It can't. That's not what I feel. Oh, don't let this happen now.

"God, she can't die." Blair's head snapped up when she realized she'd spoken aloud. Her eyes met Stark's in the mirror. There was sympathy and kindness there. Probably more than she deserved. "Can you find someone to tell me what's happening to her?"

"Yes, ma'am," Stark said softly. "I'll do that."

❖

Seven hours later, Blair wakened to the muted sound of voices just outside the lounge where she had been sleeping on the sofa. Quickly, she rose, hurried to the door, and looked out into the hall. Two women, neither of whom she recognized, were absorbed in conversation, their expressions intent, their voices low and serious. One was clearly a medical person, probably a surgeon if her blood-splattered navy scrubs were any indication. The other, an elegantly beautiful woman who looked heart-stoppingly like Cam, looked over at that moment and met Blair's eyes.

"Ms. Powell?"

"Yes," Blair said, walking forward.

"I'm Marcea Casells, Cameron's mother."

"Blair Powell." Blair took the offered hand and found herself holding it instead of returning the handshake. Surprisingly, Cam's mother's hand was warm whereas her own felt frozen. "I'm so sorry for what's happened."

"The surgeon," Marcea said, indicating the disappearing form of the woman with whom she had just been speaking, "says that Cameron is stable for the moment. We have reason to be happy."

"Thank God," Blair whispered. "I was so afraid…"

"Yes. I can imagine." Marcea folded Blair's hand into the crook of her elbow, drawing her near. Her gentle eyes skimmed Blair's drawn face, noting the hollows beneath her eyes and the faint tremor in the fingers resting on her arm. "You were there? You saw?"

For an instant, everything returned full force, and Blair shuddered. "Yes, I was there. She…it was supposed to have been me, apparently."

When she looked at Cam's mother, she couldn't hide the guilt. She said again, "I'm so sorry."

"I don't believe that Cameron would want you to be," Marcea said kindly as they settled side by side on the sofa in the lounge. Grant stood by the doorway and another agent stood just outside in the hall opposite the lounge. "I'm certain she would say she was only doing her job."

A smile flickered across Blair's face even as her eyes filled with tears. "Yes," she whispered. "I'm quite sure she would."

"We should be able to see her in a few minutes."

"I won't take any of the time you'll want to be with her," Blair said. "If you could just tell me… how she is."

Marcea studied the president's daughter carefully, unable to overlook the pain swimming in her eyes. "I'm sure she'll want you to be there."

❖

Thirty-six hours later, Cam's recovery was still not assured. She was barely conscious, and intermittently her vital signs had become unstable, requiring supportive measures.

Blair sat by the bed in one of the two private rooms on either end of the intensive care unit. She stroked Cam's pale cheek lightly as she watched for any sign of awareness. Her heart raced when Cam's lids fluttered, then opened briefly. Cam's dark eyes, usually so sharp and sure, were dulled with pain and drugs.

"Cam, you're going to be all right." Finding Cam's hand, Blair lifted it to her lips, whispering softly against her skin, "I need you. Hold on…please."

"Hurts…"

"Shh, I know, love, I know."

At the sound of movement behind her, Blair turned quickly, her eyes meeting Mac's. She was tired beyond fatigue, stretched to breaking with fear, bleeding in some deep place that had not bled since her mother died. It seemed that everything that mattered to her was right here in this still room. She was drowning in the unnatural silence broken only by the even more unnatural sound of life reduced to mechanical vibration and monotonous beeping. "Leave us alone, please."

"You need to get some rest."

"No. Not yet. They said another twenty-four hours before they were sure…"

Gently, he persisted, "Making yourself ill won't help…"

"It helps *me*. I can't leave her."

"I'm sorry," Mac said as kindly as he could. "We need to move you to a protected location."

"No."

"Ms. Powell, I'm truly sorry. The shooter is still at large, and we simply can't provide proper security here. The chief of staff just called me again."

Wearily, Blair nodded, because she couldn't fight everyone. "Give me one more minute, please."

"Of course."

Alone once more, Blair leaned over Cam's still form and kissed her.

Cam had no memory of the ambulance ride, of the frantic forty-minute resuscitation in the emergency room, or of the first twenty-four hours in the intensive care unit with a tube in her trachea delivering oxygen and two larger tubes in her chest removing blood and tissue fluids. A machine breathed for her; she could neither move nor talk. Occasionally, she would register some small sensation—sound, a light, someone touching her. Always, there was a soft voice, murmuring words of consolation that had no meaning, but were strangely soothing.

Pain was a distant thunder, rolling slowly through the landscape of her awareness, ever present. Whenever she would begin to awaken, it would be there, making her moan with its relentless onslaught.

Can't you give her something, for God's sake? She's suffering.

The voice was so familiar, yet the face so elusive. Once, Cam opened her eyes and was certain that the tear-stained face bending near her own was Blair's. But that couldn't be right, could it? The next time she opened her eyes, she was lucid enough to realize it was a nurse.

Snippets of conversation floated over her head, but despite her desperate attempts to make sense of what was happening, there were huge gaps in her consciousness, destroying any sense of reality. People touching her, turning her, tending to her. The single touch that anchored her the most, however, was a gentle hand that seemed to enclose hers for hours on end. Whenever she could summon the will, Cam squeezed the fingers clasping hers, and the voice would come again, murmuring tender words of love and encouragement in her ear.

"Who…are…"

"It's all right, love, don't try to talk now."

"Stay…"

"I will."

❖

Cam lay quietly, eyes closed, taking stock of her situation. Most of the tubes she had been dimly aware of the last few days were gone. The noise level around her had also decreased, and she sensed that she wasn't in the intensive care unit anymore. A hand slowly stroked her hair. She opened her eyes and focused on the woman beside her. She was surprised at how bright the sunlight filtering through the window appeared.

"Hello, Mother." Cam reached for the fingers softly brushing her cheek, amazed, and not a little frightened, to discover how difficult a task that was. She hoped she didn't look as weak as she felt.

"Hello, Cameron, darling."

Cam blinked again in the sunlight, and then she saw the hint of movement, the glint of metal, and it all came back to her in a rush.

"Blair!" Panic gripped her. "Is she all right? Was she hurt?"

Anxiously, she tried to sit up and found that she was unable to raise her shoulders more than a fraction of an inch. The pain she had been living with for days suddenly coalesced into a bright hot lance of fire searing through her chest. "Oh…oh," she gasped involuntarily, collapsing against the pillows again. Sweat broke out on her face, soaking the sheets instantly. "God."

"Lie still, Cameron," her mother admonished firmly. "Ms. Powell is fine. She wasn't injured. In fact, you were the only one—"

she hesitated for a moment, steadying her voice. "You were the only one who was shot."

"Where is she?" Cam persisted hoarsely, struggling to contain the wave of nausea that followed on the heels of the agony in her chest. She remembered the soothing caresses and soft voice, the gentle words of love. *Had* that been Blair?

"They took her somewhere safe," Marcea responded, too concerned by the wash of sweat across her daughter's face to explain that Blair had not gone willingly or before she had nearly collapsed from exhaustion herself. "Don't talk, Cameron. It's too soon."

Cam closed her eyes briefly, sapped by the effort to sit up. Despite her fatigue, she felt peaceful and content. Blair was safe. Sleep was coming quickly, but she needed to know. "Who's in command? Who's looking after her?"

"I believe it's a gentleman named Macintosh, or something like that."

Mac. Good. He won't let anything happen to her. Reassured, secure in that thought, she closed her eyes and escaped the pain.

Marcea Casells looked down at her sleeping child. She thought of the other young woman who had spent so many hours beside this bed, holding her daughter's hand, stroking her hair, whispering to her in low, loving tones. She knew whatever battles her daughter had been waging, those long dark hours had been made lighter by Blair's presence.

She wondered if either of them understood the depth of their connection, which perhaps could only be appreciated by someone standing outside the circle of their intimacy. She knew her daughter's sense of duty well enough to know that Cam would not have allowed anything to transpire between them. It was just as clear to her that despite their best intentions, something very significant had. Wearily, she made her way down the hall to the pay phone. Reading from the slip of paper in her hand, she punched in the numbers that had been written there for her.

"This is Marcea Casells," she began when a male voice answered. She was told to wait a moment, and then a woman spoke anxiously into the phone.

"Yes? Is she—"

"She's awake. Weak, but otherwise she seems to be quite all right."

A moment of silence, then a voice that shook slightly. "Thank you so much for calling me."

"Of course." Marcea hesitated a second, then added, "She asked about you immediately."

Blair took a sharp breath. Leaving Cam, still uncertain as to her fate, had been the hardest thing she'd ever done. She'd felt like she was leaving her heart behind. *God, how I wanted to be there when she woke up!*

"Ms. Powell?"

"Yes, I'm here. Could you tell her—tell her I…" Blair halted in confusion. Cam would never believe her. Not after seeing her in the bar, watching her with another woman, not knowing that the stranger had been no more than a substitute. And then they'd fought, just hours before the nightmare had begun.

"I think you'll have to tell her that yourself," Marcea said gently into the silence, "when the time is right."

"Yes, of course," Blair said swiftly, her emotions now firmly under control. She thanked Cam's mother and hung up the phone. She turned away, knowing that there would never be a time when she could share with Cam what was in her heart. But she *could* see that Cam was never hurt because of her again.

❖

"Did the doctors say I couldn't return to active duty?" Cam asked at length. "Are you trying to tell me I'm being retired?"

"Hell, no," Assistant Director Stewart Carlisle asserted. "We can't fire you after the president practically gave you a medal."

"A paper honor. No big deal." She shrugged, then gritted her teeth. The slightest movement hurt. "Then what the hell is going on, Stewart? There's an UNSUB still at large and a job that needs to be done. They said I'd be down for a few months. It will be less, I guarantee it."

Carlisle looked out the window, searching for words, wishing he had a different answer. He didn't understand it, but it wasn't his call. Cameron Roberts was a hero throughout the agency and had been publicly commended by the president. She had done, without hesitation, what each of them had secretly asked themselves if they could do. She had been willing to die in the line of duty. They didn't come any better than her. What he had to say didn't make any sense.

"The doctors said you'll be fine. That's not the problem." He turned to look her in the eye, because she deserved to get it head on. "Blair Powell personally requested that you be relieved of command. She went over everyone's head. There's not much we can do about that."

"I see," she said in a voice totally devoid of emotion. Her right hand gripped the covers tightly, but otherwise she lay without moving. She had been hoping—*What you were hoping doesn't matter anymore. It wasn't her. You were wrong.*

Blair hadn't come to the hospital; Cam hadn't expected her to. Once she'd been able to take calls, Mac had filled her in. The team had sequestered Blair after the shooting for her own protection, and the plan was to keep her out of public view for a while. As the days had passed, though, Cam *had* wondered at the absence of any message from her. Now she understood the silence.

Blair had finally managed to escape at least one of her bonds. *She's free of me.*

"Look," Carlisle said briskly, unnerved by the silence. "Once you're cleared for duty, you'll have your pick of assignments. Hell, after what you did, you could sit out your days until your pension on a some fancy island for all anyone would care."

"Right. Thanks for coming, Stewart." Her face was a careful blank, but a shadow of grief passed through her eyes.

When Carlisle left her room, Mac was waiting in the alcove down the hall.

"How did she take it?"

Carlisle studied Mac carefully, wondering how much he could disclose. What he saw was a look of genuine concern and something more, something that looked a lot like sympathy. "She took it well. She didn't argue or put up a fight."

"Uh-oh," Mac said hollowly.

"Yeah. Worries me, too." Stewart didn't know what to make of the way she'd looked when he'd left the room. She was staring at some distant point, so still he could barely see her breathing.

"Yeah, well, she'll be fine. She always is," Carlisle said sadly.

Mac wasn't nearly so sure. Taking a deep breath, he went to pay his respects to the woman he was about to replace.

Chapter Fourteen

Four months later, Cam was deemed fully recovered physically and cleared to go back to work. She finished rehab ahead of schedule, as predicted. She also completed her mandatory psychiatric counseling, and just as she had after Janet was killed, she passed without difficulty. One thing she was expert at concealing was her emotions. No one seemed to notice the sorrow in her eyes, and if they did, they didn't comment. No one ever doubted Cameron Roberts's ability to do the job. It was almost as if the last half-year had never happened.

Now, as she sat in Stewart Carlisle's office in the Department of the Treasury to receive her newest assignment, it was just like it had been the day he'd assigned her to command Blair Powell's security team. It was déjà vu, but everything was different, including her. She was more alone than ever. Then at least she'd been numb. And when she'd needed contact, a brief surcease from the isolation, she'd had Claire.

That was different, now, too. When she'd sorted through her things after being released from the hospital, she came across the note Claire had left the last night they'd spent together, a lifetime ago. It had been in the pants pocket of her trousers since the day she'd been shot.

C, I have a feeling I won't be hearing from you for a while. I'll miss you, more than you know. If ever you need – anything, call me. C.

Cam had never called, knowing that what she needed, Claire could not give her. Not this time. After Janet had died, she'd lost herself in work, and when she'd needed something to ease the sadness and the guilt, Claire had helped her forget. Blair Powell was impossible to forget, and no one else's touch was going to satisfy the longing.

"So," Carlisle finished, watching her carefully. She seemed distracted, and that was unusual for her. But, hell, she'd earned a little slack. "Regional director, back in investigations. Right up your alley."

"What's the catch?" Cam asked mildly, willing herself to focus on what he was saying. *This is what I'm good at. What I wanted—before New York. Before Blair. I should be glad. Why don't I feel anything at all?*

"No catch. Your team will be investigating the counterfeit money laundering operation in South Florida. You'll liaise with DEA."

"Just like always," Cam said grimly. "Fine. I'll need a few weeks on the ground to get a sense of the team and the network they have going—check out the contacts and the informants, that sort of thing."

"You're the regional director," he said with a laugh. "You don't need to do field work."

Cam eyed him steadily. "I'm perfectly fit for duty. And I know what it takes to do the job, Stewart."

"Understood. But being shot twice in the line of duty is enough for any agent," he commented dryly. "Despite the fact that you're a hero, you'll give us a bad name."

"Heaven forbid," Cam said with a perfectly straight face.

"Well, just keep your ass out of the line of fire," Stewart said roughly. He looked to the papers on his desk, indicating that their obligatory meeting was over. He was surprised when she spoke.

"How is Mac handling the other detail?" she asked quietly. She hadn't meant to ask, but she hadn't heard anything about the apprehension of the shooter. Which meant Blair was still at risk. It was on her mind. All the time.

He was almost successful in hiding his surprise. This was the first time she had referred in any way to her previous assignment. He contemplated issues of security for a few seconds. *What the hell, she deserves an answer.*

"No major security breaches, if that's what you mean. Phillips is very circumspect with his reports, but I gather that the subject is still throwing up roadblocks whenever possible." He regarded her intently for moment. "As a matter of fact, I could use a straight briefing about what's going on up there. You're not due to report to this new post for almost a week. How about dropping in on Mac and getting the real story?"

Cam stiffened, her displeasure clear. "I'm not going to spy on another agent. Mac Phillips is perfectly capable. I'm sure if you speak with him, he'll tell you whatever you need to know."

"Hell, I'm not doubting Mac's ability. But I'm no fool either. I know damn well that he's soft-pedaling the details of the reports to protect Blair Powell. Remember, the guy who tried to kill her is still out there, and we couldn't keep her secluded forever." He played his trump card, because he was a politician, and he knew that only an appeal to duty would sway her. "She's still in real and imminent danger. Any information can only help us. If you don't want talk to Mac, talk to her."

"No way." Cam stood abruptly, then turned and strode purposely toward the door. Blair hadn't called, and Cam hadn't contacted her. There was no reason to. Her job was done. Their association was history. It didn't matter that she rarely passed a day—hell, an *hour*—without thinking of her. Blair Powell had never thought of her as anything more than an obstacle to her freedom. She wasn't going to intrude on Blair's life now. Blair would hate it, and seeing her would...hurt.

"Roberts," he said in that soft, deadly tone that meant he was completely serious. "Don't make me pull rank. Just find a way to do it that you can live with. Five days. Then I'll expect to hear from you."

She didn't answer. She didn't trust her voice not to tremble.

❖

As she drove through the Lincoln Tunnel into Manhattan, Cam reminded herself that she was in New York City for the sole purpose of attending the opening of her mother's gallery exhibition. It was the first East Coast showing for Marcea in a number of years, and Cam knew it would please her mother for her to be there. She had absolutely no plans to visiting the command center, and certainly no intention of seeing Blair Powell. She reminded herself of these facts every few minutes, whenever she found her mind drifting to the images that she *thought* she had successfully eradicated. Images of Blair in a smoky bar, her hair wild and her hunger unleashed; Blair, elegant and cool on the dais of the parade route; Blair, vulnerable and weary in the hospital after the ski accident. Every memory of her triggered a kaleidoscope of wistful wanting and explosive desire.

God damn it. She forced her concentration back to the congested city traffic, grateful for something, anything, to distract her from the aching need that was never far from the surface of her consciousness.

She allowed the attendant at the Plaza to valet park her car and gave the bellman her luggage to bring up to her penthouse suite. She wasn't traveling on company time and felt no need to account for her expenditures. In fact, she felt unaccountable to anyone for the first time in her adult memory. She was between assignments, and despite Stewart Carlisle's edict, she would not be performing any duty for the United States of America for the next five days.

She signed in, and, as soon as she was alone in her suite, showered off the drive's dust and grit. She had an hour and a half until the evening opening of her mother's show. Standing naked before the bathroom mirror, trying to tame her unruly waves into position, she surveyed her image unemotionally. Her thick black hair had new touches of gray at the temples. Despite the lengthy convalescence, with vigorous physical therapy and compulsive workouts, she'd maintained her muscle mass and strength. She was sinewy and taut. The only visible difference was the scars on her torso from the bullet wound, the surgical incisions, and the multiple tubes that had been necessary to reinflate her lungs. She looked at herself dispassionately and wondered for a moment how she would appear to another. She dismissed the thought quickly. It was a moot point.

She absentmindedly went about the process of dressing. She did not glance at her reflection again, knowing that the black silk jacket and trousers were perfectly tailored for her, that her shoes were impeccably shined, and that the French cuffs of her white starched shirt were exactly the right length. When the driver let her out in front of the address she had given him, she knew that she was precisely on time. Everything in her life was exactly as it should be—predictable, ordered, and under control.

The room was already full when Cam entered, as she expected it would be. The crowd had overflowed the first level up the stairs to the second floor of the gallery, a noisy mass of murmuring critics, artists, and members of the press. Cam accepted a glass of wine from a passing waiter and began a slow tour of the area, stopping to study each new canvas. It had been a long time since she had seen so many of her mother's works in one place, and she had not seen any of her most recent creations. The hallmark characteristics of her mother's style were clearly evident, but Cam was surprised to find that the paintings seemed calmer at their core, with less of the pain that had been so evident in the early years following her father's death. *Maybe time does heal. I hope so for her sake.*

Eventually, Cam heard her mother's distinctive voice, and she gravitated toward it. Marcea, tall like herself, was visible despite the crowd of people around her. She appeared relaxed, although there was a light in her eyes, apparent even at a distance, which spoke of exhilaration. *She's talking about what she loves.*

Then Cam heard another voice that drew her up short. Blair was standing next to her mother. Heart pounding, Cam felt as if someone had struck her hard enough to drive the breath from her body. For an instant, her mind was numb, then every sensation she had been trying to suppress regarding Blair Powell flooded back. Her pulse raced, her blood pounded, and her hands began to tremble.

Blair looked up and their eyes met. Then Blair's lips parted in surprise, her blue eyes widened, and a faint blush stole across her cheeks. She took an involuntary step forward, as if intending to rush toward Cam, then halted uncertainly. They stared at one another as moments passed.

Surprisingly, Blair regained her composure first. She threaded her way through the intervening crowd until she stood in front of Cam. She tilted her head and smiled wistfully. "How are you, Commander?"

Cam finally found her voice and answered with as much control as she could muster. "I'm fine, Ms. Powell."

Blair studied her carefully. Physically, she did look fine, and as strikingly handsome as ever. But there was a strange flatness in her gaze and an emptiness in her voice, as if something vital was missing. Instinctively, Blair touched her arm. She was shocked to feel her tremble. Her sources had told her that Cam had recovered completely, but now she wasn't so sure. She had never seen her even the least bit unsteady. "Are you sure? Cam?"

Cam nodded curtly, trying to hide her turmoil. The place where Blair's hand rested was all she could feel. She had tried so hard to forget her, and just one brief touch brought back all the wanting. She finally managed to answer evenly, "You have me at a disadvantage. I didn't expect you. I didn't see any of our people outside or in the crowd."

"Ever observant, Commander. They're in a car parked across the street." When she saw Cam frown, she smiled faintly and added, "Everyone here has been thoroughly prescreened. I'm quite safe."

"Forgive me." Cam finally smiled and tried to relax. "It is not my place to question these things any longer. I should speak to my mother." She turned to leave, needing to escape from the penetrating blue gaze and the searing touch on her arm. "It was good to see you again, Ms. Powell."

"Wait, Cam," Blair said impulsively. When Cam turned back to look at her questioningly, she continued, "I wanted to say…thank you. It is so inadequate, but…I…thank you."

Cam spoke without thinking. "Blair, you don't need to thank me. God…I couldn't have stood it if anything had happened to you."

"Why do you think I would feel any differently?" Blair questioned urgently, her throat closing on the words. She had struggled for so long with her worry and fear and guilt. Blair grasped her hand, and their fingers entwined instinctively. "I was so frightened. I couldn't bear that you might die because of me. *For* me. I never wanted anyone to do that, especially not someone I…care for."

"Please, Blair," Cam murmured, catching a glimmer of tears on her lashes, "don't. You were not responsible."

"No?" Blair shook her head, her voice a mere whisper. "I'm not so sure."

"I should go," Cam said desperately. God, she wanted to hold her, and she couldn't keep denying it. Being this close to her, touching her, was bringing her carefully constructed barricades tumbling around her. When they'd been separated, she'd been able to convince herself that she didn't want her, didn't need her. Because it was impossible—impossible for so many reasons, not the least of which was that Blair obviously did not want her. But she had lied to herself. And now she was very much in danger of saying, or doing, something she would regret. "Please, excuse me."

When she turned to leave, Blair stopped her with a hand on her arm.

"No, *I* should go. You came to see your mother. She'll be devastated if you leave now." Blair tried unsuccessfully to hide her bitter disappointment. She had come close to telling her things she didn't want to acknowledge, even to herself. She should have known there was too much standing between them for that to be anything but foolish. She didn't think she could tolerate being in the same room as Cam, not with the distance between them so great, not with the wanting so keen it was an ache in her depths. For the briefest of instants, Blair laid her fingertips on Cam's chest. "It was good to see you again, too, Commander. Please know I'll never forget you."

And with that, she was gone.

❖

"What a surprise!" Marcea kissed her daughter on both cheeks, then grasped her hands and leaned back, surveying her fondly. "I'm so glad you came, Cameron. I know these aren't your favorite events."

Cam tried to smile, still shaken by her encounter with Blair. "I'm sorry it's been so long. I'm so happy for you."

"You look well."

"I'm fine, thanks." Cam couldn't help but look toward the door. She couldn't see her anywhere. *She's gone. Christ, but it hurts.*

Marcea detected the turmoil in her daughter's eyes and glanced briefly around the room. She did not see Blair. She hesitated for a moment, and then spoke gently. "Have you seen Blair?"

"Yes." Cam swallowed, replying softly, "We just spoke."

"She's a remarkable woman." Marcea sensed her daughter's struggle for composure. "A gifted artist."

"She's…" Cam faltered. "She's extraordinary."

Going on instinct, Marcea continued, "I'm sure no one told you, Cameron, but Blair stayed by your side for almost forty-eight hours after you were injured. She refused to leave until your people forced her."

Cam gasped and closed her eyes briefly. "It *was* her."

"Yes," her mother said simply.

Blair. It was Blair's voice I heard. Blair's hand I clung to.

And suddenly, right now, that was all that mattered. Cam met her mother's gaze, a faint stirring in her heart. She smiled, her eyes flickering with a light that had been absent for months. "Thank you for telling me that. Thank you."

Marcea had no time to answer before Cam turned and swiftly made her way through the crowd and out the door.

CHAPTER FIFTEEN

"Commander!"

"*Ex*-Commander," Cam said with a tired smile.

Mac glanced at the clock. 0005. Too late for a social call. "How can I help you, Commander?"

"I need to see her, Mac," Cam said, much more calmly than she felt. "I've been leaving messages at her apartment for hours."

Mac didn't even consider not telling her. "She's downtown. We know where she is, but it's awkward to make contact at the present time."

"In a bar." It was a statement, not a question. She didn't need an interpreter. She knew what Blair did to fill her solitary hours. She took a deep breath, trying to ignore the sinking sensation in her stomach. "Or has she already gone home with someone she picked up?"

"No," Mac hastened to clarify. "She didn't. She's still at the bar." He didn't think it was his place to tell the commander that this was the first time in months that Blair had been out to a club, or that she seemed to have given up her penchant for one-night stands.

"I'd appreciate it if you'd tell me which one," Cam stated quietly. "I know it's against regs, but—"

"The Hudson Arms," Mac said without hesitation, indicating one of the seedier bars deep in the village. "Uh, Commander, Stark is inside somewhere."

Meaning Stark will recognize me if I show up, and he's worried about my reputation.

"Thanks, Mac," Cam said, not caring in the least what anyone thought.

Thirty-five minutes later, Cam was standing at the bar, scanning the room. It was Friday night and the club was crowded with women of all ages, mostly in denim and leather. She didn't see

Blair immediately, but she did see Stark. Stark saw her too, although the young agent, looking completely at home in leather pants and a shirt open far enough to be eye-catching, did not acknowledge her in any way. A slight raise of the eyebrow was all that indicated she had spotted Cam.

She's getting good.

Then, Cam forgot about Stark, stopped searching faces, and let her senses engage the room. Closing her eyes, she felt the damp heat of many bodies brushing against her skin; smelled the mixture of alcohol, cologne, and sex in the air; heard the murmur of the hunt swirling all around. She sensed the ultimate huntress in the crowd the way prey senses the predator. Then Cam opened her eyes and saw Blair.

She never got over the quick jolt of pleasure that always accompanied the first sight of her. There was no one else to compare; Blair was exquisite—tawny blond hair, taut golden body, and the piercing gaze that systematically evaluated, then discarded, possible partners.

Tonight, though, Blair seemed oddly removed from the searching crowds that surrounded her. She stood alone, her expression remote, almost bored. As Cam watched, a dark, lean warrior in tight blue jeans and a sleeveless black T-shirt approached Blair, leaned close, and appeared to whisper something in her ear. Cam didn't need to see any more. She knew exactly what would happen next, and just how quickly the capture would be consummated.

Not this time.

Cam moved quickly, reaching Blair just as the dark-haired youth lifted a hand to brush Blair's cheek.

"Sorry." Cam grasped the woman's wrist, firmly but not harshly. "She's not available."

"Oh yeah?" The younger woman attempted a show of bravado, stiffening as she took in Cam's stony expression. "Since when?"

Cam's voice was low, but steely. "Since right now."

There must have been something in Cam's demeanor that warned of impending danger, because the other woman hesitated for a brief second, then melted swiftly into the crowd.

"Thanks a lot. You just ruined my evening," Blair said by way of greeting. Secretly, she was shocked to see Cam, and even more at a loss to understand her actions. It was the first time Cam had ever overtly interfered with Blair's private activities. As if that weren't enough, there was a coiled tension in her ex-security chief's body that was impossible to miss. If she didn't know better, she would've thought it was sexual.

"Ruining your evening was *not* what I had in mind," Cam rejoined, moving close enough that their thighs touched. She traced the line of Blair's jaw with one finger, her eyes darkly dangerous. "Far from it, in fact."

"Oh?" Blair caught her breath at the caress, so light that it was barely perceptible. The touch was so exquisite that she felt it in her bones, and she was instantly wet. Determined to maintain control, she asked in an exaggeratedly even voice, "Just what *did* you have in mind, Commander?"

"I'll show you." Cam reached for her hand and tugged. "Come with me."

Blair hesitated, unable to think with Cam suddenly so close. "No, wait, we can't. Stark is on the other side of the room."

"It won't be the first time she's seen you leave somewhere with a woman." Her tone was flat, impatient. She saw no point in pretending that they both didn't know what had happened in the past. And she couldn't wait any longer. Didn't *want* to wait.

"Yes, but it would be the first time she's ever seen me leave with *you.*"

"Don't let it concern you." Cam's face softened as she linked her fingers gently through Blair's, but her tone was urgent. "It doesn't bother me. Please—"

Cam tugged on Blair's hand again, drawing her into the crowd, and Blair felt strangely powerless to resist—perhaps because she had absolutely no desire to. She followed, unprotesting, outside into the dark night. Once in Cam's car, they were both silent, and the silence persisted until Blair stood in the hotel room, looking around uncertainly. She slipped out of her coat and watched Cam toss her own on the couch. Cam looked so good in a polo shirt and jeans, she felt another wave of arousal flood her thighs. *God. I can't stand this.*

"I have no idea why I'm here," Blair said, almost pleadingly. *I want you so much.*

Cam turned, their bodies mere inches apart. "Don't you?"

"No," Blair whispered, her throat suddenly dry. The breath caught in her throat at Cam's unmistakable look of desire, and all her usual quick retorts and caustic replies deserted her. This was a new experience. She was suddenly in the middle of a scene she had not written, in a role she did not know how to play. She had only her instincts to fall back on, and the undeniable demands of her own desires. "I can only hope."

Cam put her hands on Blair's shoulders and brought her lips to within a whisper of Blair's. "Do you know how much I've missed you?"

"It's been so long," Blair murmured, her vision hazy. "I never thought—"

"God, don't you *know?*" Cam trembled with the effort to contain her raging senses. Forcing the words out through a jaw tight with need, she struggled not to yield to the ferocious hunger that crawled long her spine. "Must I tell you that I want you?"

Blair moaned, her vision dimming as the blood raced to her core.

"It *kills* me to see someone else touch you." As Cam whispered the words, she dropped her hands to Blair's hips and pulled her close. Then, with Blair crushed to her, she brought her mouth to hers, heavily, possessively, and kissed her. Groaning, she parted Blair's lips with her tongue and sought the soft inner recesses, losing herself in the consuming heat.

Blair was beyond surprise. How many nights had she lain awake, trying not to think about how much she wanted this elusive woman? How many times she had attempted to satisfy the need with her own touch? But even her familiar hands and unerring caresses could not still the longing that went far deeper than flesh.

Now it was happening, and the reality was so much more than her imaginings, she could scarcely absorb it. The core of her was melting, surging white hot and molten through her limbs. She clutched Cam's shoulders for support, uncertain how long she could stand. When Cam's probing tongue filled her mouth, she bit down hard enough to make Cam grunt, then sucked fiercely as

Cam yanked the blouse from her jeans and thrust her hands upward along Blair's ribs.

"God, yes," Blair urged, grasping Cam's wrists and pushing her breasts into Cam's palms. Moaning, she sagged as strong fingers squeezed her nipples, tugging them into screaming erectness. Suddenly, fear warred with desire. No one had touched her this way in years. She never let anyone, had never *wanted* anyone, to touch her this way. Her self-control was her armor, and she was terrified as it slipped away. She was close to totally losing control, and the small part of her mind that was still able to function rebelled.

"No," Blair gasped, yanking her mouth away.

Cam did not want to stop. She was blind with need, her blood roaring through her head, driving out all reason. With the last shred of will she had, she forced her hands to still. Lowering her head, pressing her face to Blair's neck, she grasped the soft skin of Blair's throat in her teeth. She tugged, growling, as she thrust her thigh between Blair's legs.

"Cam…"

"I've wanted you for so long," Cam gasped, her teeth on Blair's earlobe now, biting lightly as her tongue swirled over the sensitive ridges. "Please—I'm dying I need you so bad."

Blair couldn't think. Each second her body pushed closer to the edge. Dimly, she was aware of her thighs trembling as she rubbed herself against the hard muscles of Cam's thigh. A terrible pressure was building between her legs, and she whimpered as spasms began to ripple outward.

"Oh no," she gasped, her voice quite different now. Tremulous. "I'm…ready to come—"

"Oh, no you don't," Cam warned, as she lifted her up, forcing Blair to thread her legs around Cam's waist for balance. Cam held the trembling woman in her arms as she moved toward the bedroom. "I'm not done with you yet."

"I'm so close," Blair gasped, pressing her forehead hard to Cam's shoulder.

"Hold on to it as long as you can." Cam's throat was tight, her mind reeling. "God…I want to taste you first."

Blair struggled to focus on Cam's face as Cam lowered her to the bed. She looked starved, wild, fierce. That look alone was enough to send another shower of electricity down Blair's thighs. "Oh please, hurry…"

"Easy," Cam whispered, pushing Blair's sweater up, then pulling it off as Blair arched from the bed. "Now the rest."

They stripped frantically and then Blair grabbed for Cam, pulling her heavily down on top of her, scissoring her legs around Cam's thigh again. She bit down hard on the skin and muscle of Cam's shoulder as she thrust desperately along Cam's leg.

"Wait," Cam murmured, her breath hot in Blair's ear, her hands on Blair's breasts again.

"I can't, I can't," Blair gasped, her fingers digging into Cam's back. "I want to so much…oh, oh…I need to…"

Cam braced her arms on the bed, pushed herself up, and in one fluid motion slid down between Blair's legs. She wasn't thinking, she was too hungry for that. It had been so long, so very long. She slipped the palms of her hands under Blair's hips and lifted, settling Blair's legs around her shoulders. Then she took her between her lips, sucking her heat, swallowing her desire, stroking her need. She could feel Blair's clitoris stiffen and she knew that even as she began to lick her that Blair was coming. She didn't stop, even when Blair's cries dwindled to soft sobs. She kept up the motion, stroking harder, faster, until once again she felt Blair swell and throb. She drove her relentlessly, beyond caring about anything except her own wild need to consume her. Within moments, Blair trembled uncontrollably, her hands twisted in Cameron's hair.

"Oh God, it feels so good," Blair wailed, convulsing again and again.

Cam didn't move for many moments after Blair quieted. Eyes closed, she rested her cheek on the soft smooth skin of Blair's thigh, just listening to her breathe. Then, her own racing heart stilled and her lids fluttered closed as she drifted on the edge of sleep, content and completely satisfied.

Chapter Sixteen

Cam awoke with Blair slowly stroking her hair. It was dark in the room, with just a faint gray at the window hinting of dawn. The sheets were twisted about her waist, and she still lay half upon Blair's body.

"Are you cold?" Cam murmured, pulling the covers with her as she pushed upward, slipping an arm around Blair's shoulders as she moved.

"No," Blair whispered as she turned into Cam, resting her head on Cam's shoulder. There was a moment of silence as they tentatively pressed closer, each acutely aware of the other's uncertainty.

"I can't remember the last time someone made love to me," Blair finally said.

Cam could remember precisely the last time she had made love to another woman. It had been casually, as if it were only one time of many, with many more to come. She hadn't known that early morning almost a year ago that it would be the last time she would touch Janet alive.

"It's been a very long time for me, too," was all Cam said. She didn't want to explain or relive the past. It had taken until now, and this particular woman, to awaken a desire that had lain buried in pain and guilt for months. For the moment, this was enough. More than she'd ever dared hope for.

"It was so good," Blair murmured.

"Yes," Cam sighed, stroking the length of Blair's arm languidly. "You're so beautiful."

Blair wondered about Cam's past, but she did not ask. Perhaps there would come a time when she would need to know. What she needed to know of her now had begun the morning Cam had first appeared at her apartment, commanding and certain and unyielding.

Thinking of Cam that first day, so resolute and yet so strangely kind, rekindled Blair's desire.

"You're pretty fine yourself, Commander." She turned her head to softly kiss the tender skin just below Cam's right nipple. Then parting her lips, she nipped gently, eliciting a soft groan. Smiling, she waited a heartbeat, then took Cam's nipple into her mouth, teasing it with her tongue and teeth. She continued until Cam stiffened, her hips arching slightly off the bed. Blair moved lower, kissing and biting lightly along Cam's ribs, down the flat plane of her belly, until she circled Cam's navel with her tongue. Cam's hands were in her hair now, urging her downward, but Blair resisted, taking her time, wanting to be sure that she had Cam's full attention. She trailed her fingers up the inside of Cam's legs, deliberately stopping just short of the heat that radiated from her.

"Jesus," Cam gasped. "Are you going to make me beg for it?"

"That was the general idea." Blair nestled her breasts between Cam's legs. She could feel the slick warmth against her own nipples.

Cam rotated her hips, attempting to draw the teasing firmness of Blair's nipples across her clitoris. She groaned, a deep choking sound. "Just touch me a little. Please, just a little—"

Blair pressed her thumb against the ring of muscle between Cam's buttocks, not entering, but stroking over the smooth tissues until she felt Cam shudder. Running a fingertip upward through the wet, swollen folds, she whispered, "I seem to remember someone talking about waiting."

"You're killing me, I swear to God—" Cam pressed her head back against the pillows, gritting her teeth, wanting the pleasure to continue, not knowing if it she could bear it. "I might…go off… without you."

"Oh, I doubt you'll go that easily." Blair smiled, then flicked her tongue over the base of Cam's clitoris. She was rewarded with a faint sob. As slowly as she could, she circled the very edges of the engorged tissues with her tongue, entering her at the same time. Cam's muscles contracted violently around Blair's fingers, her clitoris lengthening and becoming harder still.

"Do it, please, do it, do it," Cam pleaded desperately. "I have to come."

As much as she wanted to savor every second of Cam's desire, Blair was starting to lose control herself. She had wanted this for so long, and the reality was so much more than she had imagined. Her head pounded and her thighs clenched and unclenched involuntarily. When she took Cam between her lips, she could feel an answering surge in her own clitoris. She never came without direct stimulation, but she realized that she was very nearly there just from touching Cam. She squeezed her eyes tightly and tried to focus on Cam's rhythm.

Suddenly Cam twisted on the bed, shifting so that she lay facing Blair, her head close to Blair's stomach. Fiercely, she parted Blair's legs and took her with her mouth. Seamlessly, they echoed each other's caresses, lips and hands calling and answering as instinctively as their two hearts beat in synchrony. Cam was already too close and started to come almost as soon as Blair's lips touched her. She moaned, her lips encircling Blair's clitoris, sucking hard as her breath caught in her throat. She clasped Blair's hips, pulling her even harder against her face, trying to maintain contact as her own body bucked and surged with the explosion between her legs. Distantly, she heard Blair whimper, and knew that she too had been lifted on the crest of their merging passion.

❖

When they awoke again, it was late morning.

"Mac must be worried," Cam remarked lazily, running her hands slowly up and down Blair's back. "I'm surprised he hasn't found you yet."

"He's not as good as you are," Blair said quietly.

"You should probably call them."

"Why? Stark knew I left with you," Blair observed, an edge in her voice. *I don't want this to end. I just want a few more hours of happiness.*

"I know. But they may not know that you're *still* with me, and there's no need to cause a panic."

"Always working, aren't you, Commander?" Blair sighed, because she knew Cam was right; she couldn't run any longer. She kissed Cam gently, then slipped from the bed and padded naked into the other room to make the call. While she was there, she dialed room service as well and ordered a late breakfast for them both. When she'd finished, she returned to the bedroom and pulled Cam's shirt from a pile on the floor. She pulled it on, leaving it unbuttoned. Leaning against the doorway, she observed Cam propped up on the pillows, a sheet drawn up to her waist. There were new scars, fading badges of honor that she would give anything to erase. She caught her breath, amazed at how much she wanted her.

"How long are you here for?" she asked, trying to appear nonchalant.

"Officially?" Cam shrugged, wondering at the sudden pensiveness in Blair's expression. "Another four days. I have a new assignment, and I'm supposed to report back to Washington before I start."

"And then?"

"Florida, at least until I get a feel for the territory," Cam replied. She didn't like thinking about leaving Blair, but then they weren't even supposed to have this much. She was breaking a lot of rules, most of them her own. Looking at Blair, she didn't care. For a few days, for the sake of being with her, she would forget about the rules. *Don't think about more. Christ, a few months ago she got rid of you.*

"And *unofficially?*" Blair tried to hide her disappointment. *What did you expect? That she would want more than this?*

Cam watched her carefully, still finding her expression impossible to read. "Unofficially, I'm supposed to be here observing you."

"Well, your methods are certainly unorthodox." Blair laughed, but there was an edge to her voice. She crossed her arms over her chest, feeling suddenly exposed. "I'm not complaining, of course."

"Come back," Cam said gently, holding out her hand. "I told them I wouldn't do it."

Unable to stay away from her, Blair said on the edge of the bed and rested her hand possessively on Cam's thigh. "Why not?"

"Because Mac is a good man, and I know he can do the job." Cam lifted Blair's hand to her lips and kissed each fingertip. She turned Blair's hand over and pressed her lips to Blair's palm. "And because I respect you, and I know how little privacy you have left."

"But you came to the bar last night," Blair observed quietly.

"That wasn't business." Cam pulled Blair back into bed, back into her arms. "That was personal."

Blair closer her eyes, fearful of how much she wanted to hear those words. "How personal?"

Cam's embrace tightened, and she rested her cheek against the top of Blair's head. Her voice was husky as she answered quietly, "As personal as it gets."

❖

After breakfast, Blair pulled on clothes she'd borrowed from Cam. She liked the way the worn chinos felt against her bare skin, almost as if Cam were still touching her. *God, you're so gone. And in so much trouble here.*

Suddenly at loose ends, she stood in the center of the hotel suite and regarded Cam quietly as she finished dressing. She couldn't recall the last time she had made love with a woman and still been with her the next morning. She still couldn't quite believe what had happened between them. It felt so right, and yet until twenty-four hours before, she thought she'd never see Cam again. She'd purposefully had Cam removed from her detail, because she couldn't be around her without wanting her, and that was impossible. Even more, she couldn't bear the thought of Cam ever being hurt again because of her. It would destroy her.

"What happens next?" Blair asked, surprisingly uncertain.

Cam thought of a number of replies, but decided with a sigh that only the truth would do. She met Blair's questioning gaze squarely. "In a few days, I'll be back in Washington, and then on to Florida. You'll still be the daughter of the president of the United States. I'm not sure we have much to say about what happens next."

"I have a right to a life," Blair said, her blue eyes darkening dangerously.

"I'm not done," Cam said quietly, crossing to her and putting her arms around her waist. They had just made love. She couldn't pretend it meant nothing, and she couldn't hide behind her badge and protocol where Blair was concerned. People had been doing that to her all her life. "I shouldn't even be saying this, but I want to see you again."

"It will create talk," Blair pointed out. *God, it will start a media frenzy if it gets out.*

"I know," Cam agreed. "Unless I'm assigned to your security detail, any relationship between us will be obvious, or at least suspect."

"No," Blair said with finality, disentangling herself from Cam's embrace and moving away. There were many reasons that solution was untenable for her, not the least of which was that she knew how much the professional conflict would weigh on Cam. "I don't want you on my detail."

"Yes, you made that quite clear." Cam leaned one hip against the back of the sofa, hands in her pockets, studying Blair calmly. "But it does provide good cover."

"Cover?" Blair's eyes blazed. "So I'm supposed to let you put your life in danger so I can keep my personal life private?"

"Put my life in danger?" Cam's brows arched in surprise. "That was a one-in-a-million occurrence."

"Oh, sure." Blair shook her head in frustration. "Has it occurred to you that he's still out there? And if it's not him, there will be someone else?"

"That's always a possibility. That's why you have protection." Cam heard the edge of fear in Blair's voice and added softly, "I don't want you to live in fear. You simply need to be cautious and have good people around you who know their jobs. And I know my job. The whole team does."

"Good people, yes. But not you." The memories were still too clear. The pain still too raw. "I have no intention of letting you protect me at the risk of your own safety."

"That's what I do, Blair," Cam insisted gently.

"Not for me," Blair said, the image of Cam lying so still on the sidewalk, a spreading pool of blood beneath her, still so fresh in her mind. In a softer tone, she repeated, "Not for me."

Cam didn't miss the anguish flaring in Blair's eyes. Thinking of Blair living through the shooting, knowing now that she had spent those first tenuous hours in the hospital waiting by her side, Cam's heart ached. She quickly took Blair into her arms, cradling her gently. "Hey, it's over. I'm fine."

For now. Blair kissed her firmly, a mixture of passion and relief. "And I prefer you stay that way."

"Then it appears we have a problem, Ms. Powell." Cam leaned back, arms still around her, a soft smile on her lips. "If you won't let me guard you, what excuse do I have to be with you?"

Blair took a deep breath, and then took the biggest risk she had ever taken. "How about just because you're crazy over me?"

Cam stood very still, her hands resting on Blair's waist. She thought of her career, she thought of Blair's reputation, she thought of the president's public image. All of them issues, none of them insurmountable. She couldn't walk away. It wouldn't be easy, but they could find a way. She kissed Blair gently on the forehead, and whispered, "Well, there *is* that."

Blair released the breath she had been holding and rested her cheek against Cam's shoulder. "Since the feeling is mutual, I'd say we have a plan, Commander."

"It's a beginning," Cam murmured. "But we still have a few days before I go."

"Mmm," Blair responded, thinking of exactly what she wanted to do for those four days. "I have to leave for a Southeast Asian summit meeting on humanitarian issues with my father in a few weeks. When I come back, we'll work it out." She slid her fingers down Cam's abdomen toward her belt and began to work the buckle open. "But right now, let's not talk."

Cam laughed, her heart soaring. Pulling Blair's shirt from her chinos, she muttered, "The fact that we agree is downright scary."

Blair bit her just hard enough to make her jump. "I don't want you to get used to it."

"Oh, I might…" Cam murmured, leading Blair back toward the bed. "In a century or so."

The End

About the Author

Radclyffe is the author of numerous lesbian romances (*Safe Harbor, Innocent Hearts, Love's Melody Lost, Love's Tender Warriors, Tomorrow's Promise, Passion's Bright Fury, Love's Masquerade, shadowland,* and *Fated Love*), as well as two romance/intrigue series: the Honor series *(Above All, Honor* revised edition, *Honor Bound, Love & Honor,* and *Honor Guards)* and the Justice series (*Shield of Justice,* the prequel *A Matter of Trust, In Pursuit of Justice,* and *Justice in the Shadows)*, selections in *Infinite Pleasures: An Anthology of Lesbian Erotica,* edited by Stacia Seaman and Nann Dunne (2004) and in *Milk of Human Kindness,* an anthology of lesbian authors writing about mothers and daughters, edited by Lori L. Lake (2004).

A 2003/2004 recipient of the Alice B. award for her body of work as well as a member of the Golden Crown Literary Society, Pink Ink, and the Romance Writers of America, she lives with her partner, Lee, in Philadelphia, PA where she both writes and practices surgery full-time. She states, "I began reading lesbian fiction at the age of twelve when I found a copy of Ann Bannon's *Beebo Brinker.* Not long after, I began collecting every book with lesbian content I could find. The new titles come much faster now than they did in the decades when a new book or two every year felt like a gift, but I still treasure every single one. These works are our history and our legacy, and I am proud to contribute in some small way to those archives."

Her upcoming works include the next in the Provincetown Tales, *Distant Shores, Silent Thunder* (2005); the next in the Justice series, *Justice Served* (2005); and the next in the Honor series, *Honor Reclaimed* (2005).

Look for information about these works at www.radfic.com and www.boldstrokesbooks.com.

Other Books Available From
Bold Strokes Books

Change Of Pace: *Erotic Interludes* (ISBN: 1-933110-07-4)
Twenty-five hot-wired encounters guaranteed to spark more than
just your imagination. Erotica as you've always dreamed of it.

Fated Love (ISBN: 1-933110-05-8) Amidst the chaos and drama
of a busy emergency room, two women must contend not only
with the fragile nature of life, but also with the mysteries of the
heart and the irresistible forces of fate.

Justice in the Shadows (ISBN: 1-933110-03-1) In a shadow
world of secrets, lies, and hidden agendas, Detective Sergeant
Rebecca Frye and her lover, Dr. Catherine Rawlings, join forces
once again in the elusive search for justice.

shadowland (ISBN: 1-933110-11-2) In a world on the far edge
of desire, two women are drawn together by power, passion, and
dark pleasures. An erotic romance.

Love's Masquerade (ISBN: 1-933110-14-7) Plunged into the
often indistinguishable realms of fiction, fantasy, and hidden
desires, Auden Frost discovers a shifting landscape that will force
her to question everything she has believed to be true about herself and the nature of love.

Beyond the Breakwater ISBN: 1-933110-06-6) One Provincetown summer three women learn the true meaning of love, friendship, and family. Second in the Provincetown Tales.

Tomorrow's Promise (ISBN: 1-933110-12-0) One timeless summer, two very different women discover the power of passion to
heal and the promise of hope that only love can bestow.

Love's Tender Warriors (ISBN: 1-933110-02-3) Two women who have accepted loneliness as a way of life learn that love is worth fighting for and a battle they cannot afford to lose.

Love's Melody Lost (ISBN: 1-933110-00-7) A secretive artist with a haunted past and a young woman escaping a life that proved to be a lie find their destinies entwined.

Safe Harbor (ISBN: 1-933110-13-9) A mysterious newcomer, a reclusive doctor, and a troubled gay teenager learn about love, friendship, and trust during one tumultuous summer in Provincetown. First in the Provincetown Tales.

Above All, Honor (ISBN: 1-933110-04-X) The first in the Honor series introduces single-minded Secret Service Agent Cameron Roberts and the woman she is sworn to protect—Blair Powell, the daughter of the president of the United States. First in the Honor series.

Love & Honor (ISBN: 1-933110-10-4) The president's daughter and her security chief are faced with difficult choices as they battle a tangled web of Washington intrigue for...love and honor. Third in the Honor series.

Honor Guards (ISBN: 1-933110-01-5) In a journey that begins on the streets of Paris's Left Bank and culminates in a wild flight for their lives, the president's daughter and those who are sworn to protect her wage a desperate struggle for survival. Fourth in the Honor series.